Steeped In Murder Copy

A Tawny Monroe Mystery

Natalie Saar

Contents

Chapter 1

Every year, on the first Saturday after the first day of spring, Elise Huntington-Wilbury hosted Shantytown's biggest social event of the year: the Huntington-Wilbury tea party. This peculiar event was part of the reason Elise earned her nickname: the Mad Hatter. According to town gossip, the moniker was inspired by the tea-loving character from Alice in Wonderland, but Elise's reclusive nature was the other reason she earned this nickname. Aside from this single, annual event she rarely left her hillside compound and she almost never invited anyone up.

The Mad Hatter's personal mystique combined with the town's people's curiosity about her estate made an invite to the Huntington-Wilbury tea party the hottest ticket in town. And that was really saying something in a place like Shantytown.

Despite its name, Shantytown was home to some of the wealthiest people in the world. It was nestled on the southern California coast, a halfway point between Los Angeles and San Francisco, which made it an ideal place to escape. Yet despite its famous residents, Shantytown somehow never lost its small fishing village charm.

Originally, only a handful of people settled there, and they were all fishing families. There was still a wharf in Shantytown that got a lot of use, but not nearly as much as it did in the old days. Now it was mostly artisanal chefs who stopped by to get wild-caught fish of all kinds. Because of its location on the coast, fishermen could travel a day south to the warm waters off Baja California or up toward the cooler Pacific Northwest to seek out high-ticket fish. Or they could simply stay in the rich waters right off the coast and be home with their family every night.

A few decades ago, a wealthy family was driving through Shantytown and their car tire went flat. It was an easy fix, but it made the father, Erving Wilbury, work up an appetite. So he took the family to the local diner to eat some lunch before heading on their way. The father was so enamored with the quaintness of the town, the friendliness of the people, and — at the time — the low prices of real estate that he decided to build a family vacation home there.

That's how Elise Huntington-Wilbury inherited her mansion on the hill, overlooking the entire town and as far out to sea as the marine layer would allow.

The reasons why Erving Wilbury put down sticks in Shantytown were the same reason I decided to call this place home, too.

Only three months ago I'd been working as a private investigator in Los Angeles when my most recent case took a dangerous turn and landed me in the hospital for a month with most of my bones broken.

I'd been hired to tail the husband of a woman named Svetlana, because Svetlana believed her husband Dmitri was cheating on her. If I could find evidence, then she could use it as grounds to get a divorce. But one night after a few drinks, Svetlana let it slip to the girlfriend of one of her associates that she'd hired me.

This information made it through the grapevine and a mobster named Ivan Ivanoff beat me so badly that I was bed-ridden in a hospital for weeks. Svetlana felt terrible about what happened and visited me regularly, assuring me she'd take care of all of the medical bills.

While that was a financial weight off my mind, the gravity of the situation made me realize that I needed to make a life change. The deeper you got in the P.I. world, the more you exposed yourself and the more dangerous it got.

I knew it was time to leave Los Angeles. Well, as soon as I could get out of this hospital bed.

I wasn't sure where I'd go though. I knew I wanted something slower paced that would allow me to heal both my body and mind after that traumatic experience. When I was able to, I packed up what I owned, sold what wouldn't fit in my car, and started driving up the coast. Initially I was looking for a nice place to rest for a week or two, to calm down my nervous system and think about my future plans.

Then I stumbled on Shantytown and like Erving Wilbury, I fell in love instantly. Everything about it was different from the fast-paced, high-stress city life I had before and I found myself craving the change.

So, I rented a vacant office space with a little apartment above it and set up Tawny Monroe Fitness. Before I'd made the leap to private investigating, I got my undergraduate degree in kinesiology, and am a certified teacher of just about any physical activity imaginable. I'd even worked on a few movie sets in between P.I. jobs to help the actors train both for everyday fitness and specific stunts. I always loved helping people feel like their best, healthiest selves and was excited to get back to doing just that.

To start drumming up business, I put flyers all around town and within a few weeks I had enough local clients to fill up my calendar and more importantly cover the rent on both my studio and apartment. But it wasn't all sunshine and rainbows because my arrival meant I already had a nemesis: Duncan Harris.

Chapter 2

Duncan Harris was the other personal trainer in Shantytown, and we couldn't have been more different. Despite his boot camp-like training style, Duncan was a slim, lithe man, not buff and brawny like a bodybuilder. He was about 6% body fat and would tell anyone who would listen. His training method was to instill a mindset of deprivation as a form of pride in his clients. The more you deprived yourself of the things you wanted, the stronger you were. And for a reward, you'd get to do even more physically demanding exercise. He told his clients that whenever they skipped dessert, for example, they should reward themselves by running sprints and eating a protein bar.

My style is the opposite. A more holistic approach, focused on making sure people enjoyed the exercise they were doing, and reinforcing that letting the body move is a way of thanking it for all it does. I don't believe food is the enemy or simply calories that need to be counted.

In my experience, this approach got my clients better and more sustainable results than Duncan's "bootcamp for life" program. Over time, Duncan's clients trickled my way. To say Duncan wasn't happy about that would be an understatement.

Some of my clients like to come to my studio in town to work out. They said it helped to be in a new atmosphere, but others asked me to drive to their homes to train. Truth be told, I love it when they ask because I get to see their jaw-dropping mansions. Sometimes they even schedule group classes at someone's house who isn't a client but wants to host a fun class for their friends.

Despite visiting quite a few of the local mansions, one home I had never had the privilege of checking out was the Huntington-Wilbury estate. I'd heard all about it from my client and local best friend Jessica Harrington.

Jessica's an actress who currently holds the title of Hollywood's "*It* girl." Unfortunately this meant that Jessica found herself spending more time on-location than in Shantytown, making it harder to hang out lately. Usually we could only snatch a few minutes here and there after a workout to grab coffee and catch up.

Today however, Jessica's crazy schedule worked out in my favor. She'd driven to my studio for her training session and we went for a walk along the beach afterward and the topic du jour was the upcoming party.

The invites for the Huntington-Wilbury Tea Party were actual physical invitations. According to local lore, no one was allowed in the event without presenting theirs. Legend has it that a few years ago, the Mad Hatter's estranged husband Harold happened to come back to Shantytown on the same day as the party. Apparently, he had been traveling for months — some people say it was years — and didn't know the party was happening on that day.

The reason for his return was that his wife hadn't responded to his requests to send some of his valuables to him and he feared she was dead. But when Mr. Wilbury showed up, *he* couldn't get into his own house because he didn't have an official, physical invitation. Security had to get Mrs. Huntington-Wilbury out to the gate to confirm it was her husband before they'd let him in.

"Tawny, you have to take this invitation for the party tomorrow. Don't let it go to waste!" Jessica instructed me. I loved that there was always a bit of drama when she talked. "I'm out of town shooting my new TV show in Tulum and I can't make it."

Jessica had only lived in Shantytown for a couple of years and had already attended the event a few times, but no one was ever guaranteed an invitation. Being the hottest actress in Hollywood had its perks though, so the invitation made its way to her home.

"Don't I need to be the person who is actually named on the invite?" I looked at the invitation, turning it over in my hands, studying all of the embossed twinkling details. The cardstock it was printed on was so thick that it might have been actual cardboard. There was no risk of the invite getting lost either since it was nearly the size of a piece of notebook paper. The font was a regal script that was almost too loopy to read but I could just make out the date and the time. It indicated the party was taking place this coming Saturday at 2 p.m. sharp.

"No, don't worry about it. Having the physical invitation is the most important part," she waved off my concern. "I mean, of course there's a list, but I'll take care of changing my name to yours."

"Is there a dress code?" I started mentally cataloging everything I owned to see if I'd need to buy something new.

"Yes, but nothing written. When I was first invited I was told that the dress code was implied in the name of the event," she smiled.

"So... tea party attire? What the heck is that? Am I the only woman in the world who doesn't have a tea party section of her closet?" I was beginning to feel self conscious just thinking about it. Was that a *normal* style of dress for people to have? I was thankful that Jessica and I wore the same size, though she was a little taller than my 5'5" frame and I was a bit more muscular than her dancer's body. But I was still able to fit into most of her clothes and benefited from her hand-me-downs. That's where our physical similarities ended. Jessica had gorgeous, thick, curly black hair and a perpetual "just back from vacation" tan, whereas I was pretty... plain. Which wasn't always a bad thing, especially when my previous livelihood depended on me blending in.

Jessica laughed her light, tinkling laugh that made millions of people all over the globe fall in love with her. "No, Tawny. You crack me up! Just wear a cute sundress or something. And a fancy hat if you have one."

"Negative on the fancy hat."

"Not a problem. There's no hat requirement. But if you want one, I can bring it to you the next time we train, which I think is tomorrow, right?" She opened the calendar on her phone to check it out.

I followed suit and opened mine. "No, actually it looks like it's next week. You're on set though, aren't you?"

"Oh shoot, you're right. Duh!" She lightly slapped her forehead.

I shrugged. "So no hat I guess. Not a big deal. I'm not really a hat person."

We hugged goodbye and I drove back home to assess my wardrobe.

Since I left Los Angeles with only a few things, there wasn't much to choose from. But I made sure to bring a few staples with me, like a light blue dress with a pleated hem that I kept around for last-minute semi-formal events like this one. My favorite part was the hidden pockets. I donned the dress, popped on a pair of nude colored kitten heels, double checked that I had my invite and laid it all out for the party the next day.

Chapter 3

I woke up bright and early, excited for the party, but had to kill time so I cleaned up my studio then went for a run. Finally it was afternoon and I got into my old, black Nissan sedan. I loved my trusty car. I'd even named it: Ole Reliable. I turned the key, saying my usual prayer that it would start, and was on my way.

The road to the Huntington-Wilbury estate wound through the hills on the north side of town, which was a side that I rarely had cause to visit. That was where most of the families with the old money lived, and they almost never called for a personal trainer. Because of that, I wasn't familiar with the winding streets that led up to the mansion.

Halfway up the hill, I lost cell reception and the GPS on my phone cut out. I frantically tried to get it working but found myself swerving on the two-lane country road. There was still enough daylight to see where it led in the distance, but the sky was getting dark quickly and I didn't want to try my luck. So I turned out at the next passing zone I saw.

Not only was my phone's GPS not working, but my screen was frozen too. I was trying to pull up the list of directions and quickly commit them to memory in case it kept acting up, but nothing was working. Left with no options, I turned the phone off, hoping that a reset would at least render it usable.

While I was waiting for the screen to flicker to life again, I saw a Rolls Royce pass on my left. Then a Ferrari. I thought that these cars were too nice to coincidentally be driving by me at the same time, and I decided to follow them.

It turned out to be the right choice because as we kept going, other cars started appearing too, and soon enough I was waiting in a line of the most expensive cars I'd ever seen.

Finally my phone decided to start working, but just barely. The cell reception was in and out. So I took a quick look at the directions while I waited and committed them to memory. The line of cars moved much faster than I had anticipated, and before I knew it, I was at the gate with a big, burly security guard asking me for my invitation. I reached over to my passenger seat and picked up the thick, heavy invitation and handed it to him. He scrutinized it, then brought out a little UV light and shined it on the invite, turning it over to check both sides. Once he was satisfied it was the real deal, he turned off his light and nodded at me to go through the gate.

Moments later, a valet was opening the door for me and I was handing him the keys to Ole Reliable. I was expecting him to wince at having to drive what was easily the cheapest car here. But maybe he had an Ole Reliable in his life too, because he simply took the key and was off.

I walked up to the house, following the trickle of party-goers around the side of the house that appeared to lead to the backyard. I tried not to let my jaw hit the floor as I took in each new angle of the property. It was hard to believe something that looked like a royal palace was nestled right here and not in Europe.

As the mansion came into view, I was even more impressed than I had been by pictures. It had an old neo-classical style but somehow also looked brand new and crisp. It was more like someone plopped Buckingham Palace down right in the seaside town.

When I got to the backyard, I saw the crowd of people milling around a giant lawn area. They had some of the most beautiful dresses I'd ever seen. They weren't ballgowns but the colors and details were incredible. And almost every single woman was wearing one of those eclectic fascinators. Jessica was right, I should have made the effort to go get a hat from her house.

There were bar tables set up around the perimeter, and shorter ones that were more appropriate for a tea party in the interior of the lawn. I thanked my higher self for choosing shoes that had a wedge and not a stiletto heel that would have sunk right into the ground. Surrounding the lawn was a massive 10ft tall hedge, creating a natural border.

Before I could finish taking in the exterior, a server walked over with a tray of champagne flutes. They were filled with a glittering red drink.

"Sparkling hibiscus tea, ma'am?" he asked, extending the tray towards me.

"Thank you," I said, taking one. He nodded and walked to the next empty-handed guest. I took a sip, not knowing what to expect. I wasn't a big tea person so I didn't know hibiscus tea from Earl Grey. This tasted tart and yet somehow still sweet, like lemonade but without the lemons. The carbonated bubbles floating to the top really did give the drink the appearance of champagne. And it seemed that there were little flakes of what I assumed was edible glitter in the glass.

Surveying the crowd I was struck by the realization that I really didn't know a single person here. Since I was still relatively new to town, that wasn't entirely surprising, but I'd gotten to know a lot of the locals and assumed I'd see a few of them. That was okay though. As a former P.I., I knew how to slip into events unnoticed if I wanted to. I'd survey the area for a while and then branch out to mingle. After only a minute or two, I realized I actually *did* know many of these people but there was no way they knew me. They were some of the most famous people in the world. Bankers, CEOs, movie stars, models, tons of them all in one place. Suddenly my sensible blue dress felt very out of place.

Then I heard a familiar voice calling my name and exhaled a sigh of relief. "Tawny! Is that you?" It was my client and town gossip Lady Sinclair.

Chapter 4

Lady Sinclair was a tall, stunning former silver screen siren. She was in her '70s — though she would say she's in her '40s — and she took such good care of her appearance that it was frankly believable. She was one of Shantytown's first famous residents back in her heyday. In fact, she liked to claim that she was the one who sparked the migration of Hollywood's elite to move here, which very well may have been true. Now she spent her days making the rounds in town, checking up on the most famous or interesting neighbors, and always waiting for the movie studios to call her with a new offer.

I'm not much of a gossiper, but if there's anything I learned from my former profession, it's that being friendly with the town gossip could prove beneficial in all kinds of ways.

I turned towards Lady Sinclair and saw her making her way towards me from only a few tables away. She looked her usual elegant self in an off-the-shoulder A-line dress and short but fashionable black heels. She had on several strings of pearls and her jet black hair was straightened into a stylish bob. "It's nice to see a friendly face," I said and I meant it.

Lady Sinclair pulled me in for an embrace, giving me her customary two-cheek European greeting then said, "No offense darling, but I hardly expected to see *you* here."

"I hardly expected it too," I said. "Jessica was invited but is out of town filming and didn't want it to go to waste. So she left her invite to me."

Lady Sinclair was *not* Jessica's biggest fan, and I suspected it was because Jessica reminded her a bit too much of her golden days. But if she was annoyed at a commoner like me being here on my friend's behalf, she didn't show it. "Now that makes perfect sense and you look lovely! I've never seen you wearing anything except *athleisure* wear." She said "*athleisure*" like it was a dirty word. "Anyways have you heard what's going on? No, of course you haven't. Poor thing standing over here all alone without a friend in the world. Thank God I spotted you. But as I was saying — the news. No one has seen Elise anywhere."

"Is that odd? Maybe she wants to make a grand entrance?" I offered. It wouldn't be the first time that someone put off their guests by arriving late in order to have all eyes on them.

"She *abhors* grand entrances," Lady Sinclair explained. "She thinks they're grotesque. No, she prefers to mingle from the very minute her party starts. Actually, Elise's parties are the only ones I show up to on time because I know how much it means to her. But I've been here for hours, and haven't seen her. I asked some of the staff who were here setting up earlier and none of them remember seeing her either. She's nowhere to be found." Lady Sinclair seemed genuinely worried, not the nonchalant self she normally was when she was delivering the latest piece of hearsay she'd picked up.

Just then there was a blood-curdling shriek coming from somewhere in the distance. Lady Sinclair's head turned so fast to see what caused the scream that she reminded me of the movie "The Exorcist." The entire party fell nearly silent apart from people muttering and looking around, trying to figure out where the noise came from and who made it.

Then a woman in a frilly pink tea dress burst out into the yard where everyone was standing and staring at her. The woman didn't seem to notice and kept screaming, clearly in shock. After a few moments, she formed some words and managed to shout "She's dead!"

Chapter 5

Before I could blink, Lady Sinclair had grabbed my hand and was leading me over to the woman who had a steadily growing crowd of party-goers around her. That didn't stop Lady Sinclair though, who was already moving towards the screaming woman so fast that I was nearly jogging, trying to keep up.

"Move! Out of my way!" Lady Sinclair barked, and to my surprise everyone listened, like she was Moses parting the Red Sea. She finally let go of my hand once we pushed our way to the front. She took the woman into her arms, hugging her while the woman broke down in sobs.

"Melinda! Who is dead? What did you see?" Lady Sinclair asked.

"It's Auntie! She's just... lying there!" Melinda choked out between gasps for air. This woman was clearly distraught. Even the best actor couldn't pull off a performance like this. I wasn't sure who "Auntie" was but I had a guess based on everyone's reaction.

"Where, Melinda? Where is she?!" Lady Sinclair asked with all of the emotion you'd expect from an Academy Award nominee. Now I knew the woman's name — Melinda.

"In there," Melinda pointed to a gap between two of the humongous hedges behind her. Her finger was shaking. I wasn't sure where the opening led, but I was sure that I was about to find out.

"Take us there," Lady Sinclair said, releasing Melinda from her embrace, and grabbing my hand again, indicating that I was coming with them.

As we walked towards the gap in the hedge, Melinda said, "I'll try and find my way back. I was so rushed trying to get out I'm not sure if I —"

"Just hurry!" Lady Sinclair shouted. "There may still be time to help her!" Then she turned to address the crowd, "And someone call 9-1-1!" She shouted. She didn't wait for a response before following Melinda who had pulled herself together enough to walk, but I could hear her quiet sobs.

"My dear, you do know you can breathe better and we can move faster if you stop crying, don't you?" Lady Sinclair gently chastised Melinda.

"You're right. I'm sorry, I'm just so —" Melinda was on the verge of breaking into heavy sobs again and completely halting our progress, when Lady Sinclair commanded, "Not. Right. Now. Melinda."

Melinda took a deep breath and nodded in agreement, then continued to lead us through what I now realized was a giant hedge maze. I'd never been in a garden hedge maze before but had always wanted to see what it was like. This obviously wasn't how I'd planned on trying it though. Now that I was in one, I had to admit it did feel pretty creepy. The hedges were so tall and the pathways were so narrow. It must take months if not years to learn how to confidently navigate around this mass of shrubs.

Every so often there were openings in the hedge wall that showcased charming little sitting areas with benches, fountains, and small gardens that were reminiscent of Queen Elizabeth's rose gardens. The English royal motif was clearly a lynchpin in the decor style here.

We were moving so quickly that it didn't take more than a minute or two before I felt completely lost in the maze. Had I been in here alone, I doubt I'd have been able to make it back out on my own. Thankfully though, it looked like Melinda had a clear idea of where we were going.

That's when it hit me that "Auntie" must have been Elise Huntington-Wilbury, the Mad Hatter. It explained why Melinda was able to navigate the maze so well. Only someone who had been in here tons of times would know where to go, especially now that the sun was going down and the shadows were getting long. It also explained why neither Lady Sinclair nor the staff had seen Elise in hours.

We came to an abrupt stop outside of one of the mini-courtyard openings. "There," Melinda pointed to the seating area in front of us. "I can't go in and see her again. Not like that," she whimpered. "Can you two go?" She was on the edge of heavy tears again.

"Of course, darling girl. Just stay here and we'll go see if anything can be done. Don't wander off though! We don't want you getting lost," Lady Sinclair said to Melinda and rushed through the opening in the hedge, pulling me with her again. Once inside I could see it was an area about 10 feet by 10 feet with a white ceramic fountain in the center and a bench surrounding the fountain. Peeking out on the ground from behind the bench on the back side were a pair of feet in black Mary Jane shoes.

Chapter 6

Lady Sinclair rounded the bench first and gasped when she saw the body of a woman lying there, white as a ghost, mouth agape. She put a hand to her chest. "I believe Melinda was right. The poor thing is most certainly dead," she whispered to me quietly enough so that Melinda couldn't hear.

"Is that her?" It was a dumb question because how many dead people could there be at one party, but since I hadn't seen so much as a picture of Elise, I couldn't be sure.

Lady Sinclair let a single tear fall from her eye, and it looked genuine, not rehearsed. My heart broke for her. After all, Elise was her longtime friend. "Yes it's her. It's Elise." Then she took a deep breath and composed herself. "Well, what are you waiting for? Get to work."

"Get to... work?" I wasn't sure what she meant. This woman had clearly been dead for quite some time, maybe hours. There was nothing left to *do* here.

"Yes, get to work!" Lady Sinclair snapped. "Start investigating!" She pointed to the body that was sprawled out on the ground in front of us.

"Oh I think I'd better leave that to the sheriff," I knew all too well how angry local law enforcement could get if I started poking around a scene before they did, especially if it meant I disturbed the body. That had gotten me into trouble more times than I cared to remember.

"Well I don't see any sheriff here, do you? But what I do see is a party full of suspects," Lady Sinclair dropped her voice and said, "Including that one over there," nodding at Melinda who was holding herself in a hug, sobs wracking her body. Her back was to us as though she really couldn't stand seeing the scene anymore.

The accusation shocked me. "You don't think she —"

Lady Sinclair raised her eyebrows. "Well she *was* the last one to see Elise and she seems a little *too* sad, don't you think? Almost... performative."

"I wouldn't jump to that conclusion yet. It must have been a horrible shock to find her aunt like this," I said, unsure why I was defending Melinda. Lady Sinclair knew more about her than I did, but I also believed she was acting like a woman who was sincerely in shock, not putting on a show. "I'll start looking around here for evidence. You take Melinda back, and don't let her out of your sight."

Even though I doubted Melinda killed her aunt, I threw that last part in there so that Lady Sinclair would feel like I was giving weight to her suspicion. She nodded, winked, and floated away towards Melinda. "And make sure someone called the sheriff like you asked!" I shouted after them. The longer it took the authorities to get here, the worse shape this body would be in.

"Consider it done," Lady Sinclair affirmed. She tapped her head indicating that she thought this was a smart plan. "I knew you'd be helpful," she said as she turned the corner out of the clearing, placing her arms on Melinda's shoulders and guiding her out of the maze.

As soon as they were gone, I regretted telling them to leave even though I knew it was the right thing to do. Since it was getting late in the afternoon and the hedges were so high that almost no sunlight reached this courtyard and the entire place was covered in shadow. The hedges also blocked out any sounds, so with everyone gone it was eerily quiet. I felt suddenly vulnerable, wondering if Mad Hatter's killer was still nearby.

I quickly reminded myself that we weren't even sure this was a murder yet and not to psych myself out. Just then the little garden lights around the edge of the courtyard flickered to life and I was able to get a better look at the scene. They weren't bright enough to get a thorough look, that would likely require flood lights or something along those lines. But these at least lit up the entire space, erasing most of the shadows that had been creeping me out.

Chapter 7

I felt a twinge of sadness looking at this mysterious woman I'd heard so much about. I'd been looking forward to meeting her and would never get the chance. She seemed to be such an enigma, and her story ended like this, falling in her own hedge maze. But I shook off all of those thoughts to focus on the task at hand.

As a private investigator, it wasn't often that I had access to a crime scene, but when I did, it was usually under circumstances like this where I happened to get there before the police. Since P.I.s don't have to get the same warrants and permissions as the police do, it's way easier for us to get a tip and act on it immediately. Sure, what I do isn't always *strictly* legal, but it's the job. Occasionally getting early access to crime scenes had landed me in hot water but most of the time I was able to take a look around and leave before anyone knew I was there.

Looking at Elise Huntington-Wilbury's body, I could see that it looked like she fell backwards, hit either the bench or the fountain, and rolled a bit onto her left side. Her expression was something between surprised and scared and I wondered how quickly she died. Usually when people had this expression it meant that they died almost instantly. Maybe someone snuck up on her and she had a heart attack. I hoped that was the case because that would be more humane than something more violent.

I saw a small pool of blood under her head and squatted down to get a closer look. Sure enough there seemed to be a wound. It was hard to see because it was at the back of her head, and I didn't want to touch the body, but the fact that she was on her side gave me a little peek. Stepping back and taking a look at the whole setup, my initial theory that Elise fell and hit her head was looking more plausible. Since the body appeared to have been here for a while, I couldn't see any other signs of bruising showing up which likely meant that there hadn't been any violence. But I had to remind myself that I didn't actually know how long the body had been here for. Those details were better left to the professionals.

Unable to discern much more without touching the body, I started to look around the courtyard. It was pristine and looked like there wasn't a single blade of grass out of place. In my experience though, first impressions aren't always what they seemed. Someone could have a squeaky clean house but still be hiding a bloody murder weapon in one of the drawers.

So I started looking for some kind of obvious clue. I knelt down to the ground, getting a good look at the lawn, specifically the perfectly pristine lawn. From this vantage point I was able to see the different directions the blades pointed. In a meticulously manicured lawn like this one, anything out of place would be obvious.

Sure enough, when I laid down at grass-level a new story unfolded. There were crushed blades all over the place, pointing this way and that. It appeared they were in the shapes of footsteps, documenting the footwork of what had taken place here. It looked like there were way more steps than Melinda and her aunt could make on their own.

I kept moving further back, crawling along the border of the courtyard, trying to see what story would unfold from different angles. Lost in the task, I suddenly heard a rustling somewhere behind me and froze in place. I wasn't sure how much time had passed, but it was definitely getting close to evening now, and the sky was dark.

It was still completely quiet in the courtyard aside from that sound. I didn't move a muscle, trying to listen for another indication of where the rustling came from. After what was probably a few seconds but felt like minutes, I didn't hear anything else and tried to calm myself down.

It wasn't easy though. The hedge maze was eerie and dulled a lot of the sound, but I still knew there were around a hundred partygoers on the other side of the hedge. And though the maze was at least half a mile of twists and turns, those people were only about 50-75 yard stone's throw away. It was possible that someone from the party got curious and wandered in here while they were looking around the grounds.

Just then there was more rustling in the hedges, and I could tell it was coming from directly behind me. I quickly jumped to the side at the same moment that a huge cat came crashing through the hedge.

It had a coat that made it look like a leopard, and while it was large for a house cat, it was still too small to be an actual big exotic cat. I'd heard about these kinds of domesticated leopard cats before but I'd never seen one in person. Though this one seemed so fierce I wasn't sure how anyone would think it was anything close to a housecat.

The mini leopard sauntered over to Elise's body, then circled it a few times before gingerly hopping on top of her and laying down, like it was some kind of guard dog.

I walked over trying to shoo it away, nervous that it was going to tip the body and contaminate the scene. But the cat hissed at me, protecting what I presumed was its owner's body, ruining any chance I had of potentially getting more information in that part of the courtyard for now.

Returning to the far corner of the clearing, I laid down again to keep studying the story the grass was laying out. That's when I noticed something that changed from before. Some of the footstep imprints were starting to disappear. I looked at the steps I'd just made while running from the cat, and those were firmly pressed in the ground. This meant the ones that were disappearing were the ones that had been here the longest. They had to belong to Elise and whoever else she'd been in here with — *if* she'd been with anyone at all. I maneuvered to the side and could see that the ones disappearing fastest did appear to be two distinct sets of footprints. One larger and one smaller. I had to get closer without disturbing the sleeping cat or I risked getting mauled by it.

I couldn't be positive of the exact shoe sizes, but it looked like the rapidly fading footprints showed an average sized set of feet that would have belonged to one person who would have been standing face-to-face with a person who had a smaller set of footprints. One quick look at Elise's black Mary Janes let me know that the smaller set most likely belonged to the victim, but I had to be sure. Crawling around like a cat myself, I crept to where the light was shining on Elise's feet and was happy to see my theory was holding up.

There were disappearing footsteps right where it looked like she'd fallen, and they were the same size as the other smaller set I'd seen. Now the question was did she fall or was she pushed?

I kept crawling around the perfect grass, trying to figure out what story it was telling me. Feeling my phone in my pocket, I pulled it out and opened the camera, trying to get it to focus on the footprints. But the combination of dim lighting, a bad phone camera, and I admit a bit of operator error, I wasn't able to get a clear, focused shot that would be helpful to anyone. I once again completely lost track of time, trying to make mental notes of as much of this evidence as I could while it was still here. Then Lady Sinclair's voice broke me out of my own thoughts.

"What on Earth are you doing down there, Tawny?"

Chapter 8

I looked up and saw Lady Sinclair standing at the opening back into the maze with her hand over her mouth, shocked to find me fully prostrate on the lawn. Melinda was standing next to her and so was a very handsome man in a sheriff's uniform. I'd never seen him before, but then again I had never needed to call the sheriff since moving here. I was suddenly very aware of the fact that I must look crazy lying on the grass like this in my formal tea dress. I picked myself up, brushing off the smallest bits of grass that still clung to me and tried not to look as embarrassed as I felt.

"I think I found something! But you have to hurry!" I announced, feeling triumphant at what I'd figured out, and just in the nick of time, too. I was also hoping this would make them — especially that cute sheriff — forget the awkward state they'd found me in.

Lady Sinclair started walking towards me and, not wanting her to disturb any of the footsteps, I yelled, "Wait! Not you." Lady Sinclair gasped, acting insulted.

"What I mean," I said in a gentler tone, trying to soothe her ego, "Is that the clue is in the grass. If you walk over here there's a chance you'll ruin it. Sheriff, I'll show you. But walk around the side to get over here, and hurry."

He did as I said which gave me even more time to take him in. This guy was the classic tall, dark, and handsome type, which also happened to be my type of guy. He was at least 6'1" and had a muscular build. When he got closer, he extended his hand to me.

"Sheriff Jeremy Jackson," he said.

"Citizen Tawny Monroe," I joked, but either the joke didn't land or he didn't think it was funny because there was no laugh. I reminded myself he was here for a job and there was a dead body over there. Maybe it wasn't the best time for flirtation.

"So what did you find?" he asked.

"I'll show you. Lay down like this," I started getting back into the position I'd been in when they'd found me in here. Sheriff Jackson followed my lead but he hesitated, letting me know he was skeptical. "C'mon, trust me," I encouraged him.

He gave in and once he was prone, he looked around. "Now what?"

"Don't you see the footprints?" I asked, a little annoyed that he hadn't noticed them as fast as I had, and started wondering if he was one of those good looking but clueless small town sheriffs or if he was actually up to the task.

Sheriff Jackson gazed over the clearing. I noticed he smelled clean, like soap and linen.

"Ahh, okay, yes I see them now. Good eye," he nodded at me, and I was glad that he was disproving my suspicions about his observational abilities. "So what do you think went down?"

"Over there by the body. You see the two sets of foot-prints?"

He squinted, "Barely but yes."

"The smaller set definitely belongs to Elise Hunting-ton-Wilbury. They're very small and if you look at her shoes they're almost certain to be a match," I explained.

"What about the others?"

"I'm not sure. It's either a woman with somewhat large feet or a man with feet on the smaller side," I explained. "But you can see they're disappearing quickly. So crawl around and make a mental note before they do."

Sheriff Jackson tapped his forehead and said, "Noted." It was cheesy, but it made me smile. Then the smile disappeared when I again remembered this was happening inches away from a dead woman's corpse.

Despite that, I could tell he had an easygoing energy that I liked. This was a tense situation where time was of the essence, but Sheriff Jackson had a calmness that made me feel less stressed about the whole thing. Then he pulled out his phone and tried to take a picture. "It won't work. I already tried it," I said. He tried anyway and said, "Confirmed. It won't focus." I started to think maybe user error was *not* the reason my pictures hadn't worked.

We both crawled around the lawn for a little while longer, looking like some out-of-place Navy Seal trainees. Once the footprints were so faint that they were barely discernible, we both stood up and walked back to Lady Sinclair and Melinda.

"What was all of that nonsense about?" Lady Sinclair seemed like she was more annoyed she couldn't hear us on the other side than at anything else. She hated being on the outside of a story.

"Tawny found footprints," Sheriff Jackson explained. "One set is Ms. Huntington-Wilbury's but it's not clear who the other set belongs to. We'll have to ask the guests their shoe sizes before we let them go."

"How very Cinderella of you," Lady Sinclair quipped.

"They're getting restless so you better hurry or I'll have an angry mob on my hands," Melinda said, sounding much more composed than earlier. Lady Sinclair must have given her a stern talking to. Or maybe she was just numb.

Instinctually I glanced down at Melinda's shoes. They were flats, which was an odd choice because they made her already somewhat large feet look even bigger. I tried not to make it obvious that I was staring, but they did look like they could be a similar size to the second set I saw in the garden. Melinda was the one who found her aunt's body after all. Then I had a realization.

"Why would *you* be the one responsible for handling your aunt's guests?" I asked.

Melinda sighed. "I'm sure you'll find this out sooner or later since she's gone now. I'm Auntie's heir. The entire estate goes to me. So I want to make sure no one ruins or breaks anything because *you*," she side-eyed Sheriff Jackson, "Won't let them leave. Have you ever seen how cagey rich people get when the cops start asking questions even if they haven't done anything wrong?"

"Sorry, but why would you get everything and not her husband? I know they're estranged, but still? Wouldn't he at least get the house or something?" I asked, both nervous I'd offend her and that she'd clam up.

"Oh, they had a prenup. He keeps his money, she keeps hers," Melinda waved it off and I was grateful that the question hadn't fazed her. "Auntie's family bought this house and she inherited it. My father was her only living sibling, and he passed away a few years ago. So the family estate goes to me."

I was putting together the pieces we had so far and glanced over at Lady Sinclair who looked like she was doing the same. But if Sheriff Jackson was thinking the same thing, his expression gave nothing away.

Melinda looked to the courtyard and her momentary steely resolve collapsed. She teared up. "I can't bear to see her like this anymore. I have to go back to the house. Please."

"Yes of course you do, dear," Lady Sinclair comforted her. "We'll go back and hold down the fort until you two are done here."

"Are you hanging back to help me?" Sheriff Jackson asked with a smile and brought me out of my thoughts. I wondered if he was happy to have *any* company or *my* company specifically. Then I mentally reminded myself to stay on task and ignore that he was very handsome and smelled good.

"Like I told you," Lady Sinclair waved him off as she and Melinda walked away, "Tawny Monroe was a private investigator. You've already seen she can be a help to you." They disappeared around the corner of the maze, back to the remnants of the party.

Chapter 9

That left me and Sheriff Jackson alone in the maze, but I wasn't concentrating on that as much as I was thinking about Melinda's shoes. They were close to the correct size and she *knew* that she was inheriting everything. A lot of times with the mega-wealthy, they don't let their heirs know who gets their money precisely because they don't want to be killed by them for it.

"So you're a private investigator, huh?" he asked.

"*Former* private investigator," I corrected, worried that this new information would turn him against me instantly.

"Well either way, Lady Sinclair is right. You could help me out some more. The Shantytown Sheriff's Station is a small one, and we only have a few people working tonight. The other two are trying to hold the partygoers until the county can send over some people to help us. So if you leave, it's just me looking everything over, and two pairs of eyes are better than one." Sheriff Jackson walked over to look at Elise's body.

"Not sure what else I can do. I've told you everything I observed," I started to say, not wanting to touch the body or be around it for any longer than I already had been.

"Don't worry. I don't want any more people around this scene than need to be. I only want to get as much info as I can before rigor mortis sets in further and we can't make any initial observations," he explained. "The county said their forensics team won't be here for at least an hour, so that doesn't leave us much time since it looks like she may have been here for a while already."

"Shantytown doesn't have their own forensics team?" I asked, a little surprised. I hadn't realized that there were so few people staffed at the Sheriff's Station.

"How often do you think we'd have cause for a full-time forensics team here?" he laughed and I felt silly for not seeing it from that perspective in the first place. "Besides, when someone rich like this dies, her insurance company will want multiple experts involved. Not just a small town cop."

"Experts," I chuckled to myself. I thought I'd said it quietly enough so he didn't hear, but Sheriff Jackson picked up on it.

"Do you have a problem with experts?" He raised an eyebrow.

"Not in general. But experts don't always live up to their name. If they did, private investigators would be out of a job," I explained. It was true! I couldn't count the amount of times a so-called expert had missed some detail or another that I had picked up on immediately. Nor the amount of times I'd been hired simply because the experts got something wrong and my clients wanted to prove the truth. At the end of the day, experts were human like the rest of us.

"You know something Ms. Monroe, —"

"Call me Tawny," I interjected. The sound of "Ms. Monroe" made me feel like there was no way he could find me attractive.

"I think we're going to get along just fine," he shot me a warm smile. The moment was short-lived though because Sheriff Jackson bent down and nudged the still-sleeping mini leopard sitting on Elise's body. It happened so quickly I didn't have a chance to warn him that bothering that cat was putting his beautiful face in the line of fire.

"Don't!" I blurted, trying to save him from the impending barrage of cat scratches, but to my surprise they never came. The cat hissed at first, annoyed at being disturbed from its sleep. Then it softened after seeing it was Sheriff

Jackson who had woken it up. To my shock, it hopped off Elise's body, and circled the sheriff's legs, purring. I couldn't believe what I was seeing.

For a second I thought the force of it jumping would make the deceased flop onto her back, further disturbing the scene, but the corpse stayed there.

"That cat nearly killed me earlier," I stared at the animal, which had transformed into a domesticated angel, curled up in Sheriff Jackson's arms.

"Guess you're just not an animal person," Sheriff Jackson shrugged. Setting the cat on the ground, it walked a few steps, stretched, then continued walking over to the hedge it had originally plunged through, until finally sashaying out of the courtyard.

Sheriff Jackson pulled out his cell phone again and turned on the camera, circling the body to get some final pictures before it was time to move Elise. It took a few minutes, but it was a thorough job. I was quiet while he worked, not wanting to break his concentration in case he had some sort of method of documenting scenes. Then he pulled a latex glove from his pocket, snapped it on, and gently pushed Elise onto her back. Now we could get a better look at what appeared to be the fatal wound on her head.

With her rolled over, it was much easier to see the blood on her left temple. This meant she probably had a quick death, and I was grateful that chances were she didn't suffer. I didn't know the woman, but I didn't like the idea of anyone enduring a long, painful death. Especially if this turned out to be an accident and not a crime. The temple was a soft spot on the skull where four skull bones met, which made it particularly vulnerable to impact. There were all kinds of stories about school fights or bar fights where one person was shocked to find they'd killed the other with a seemingly slight blow to the head, but they'd clipped the temple and their opponent's brain bumped around, killing them.

I was once again lost in my thoughts, when Sheriff Jackson asked, "What's that around her mouth? Does that look normal to you?"

He was squatting down on the ground, so I did the same, and tried to look at where he was pointing. Sure enough there seemed to be some dry, crusty drool coming out of the side of Elise's mouth. "I don't know. Could just be dried saliva. You never know what she ate right before..." I trailed off.

"Good point. I'll make sure they test it anyway, just to be sure," he said.

Then I noticed a plastic wrapper on the ground. It had been hidden underneath Elise's body before. "What's this?" I asked out loud, though the question was more to myself than Sheriff Jackson. I was used to working alone, so I had a tendency to think out loud. He reached over and picked the wrapper up with his gloves.

"I'm not positive, but I think it's —" he brought the wrapper inches away from his face. "It smells like chlorine."

"Chlorine? Like for the pool?" I asked. That was a confusing development, I thought, making sure to keep the thought in my head this time and not say it out loud.

"Yup. That's what it smells like," he dropped the wrapper in a plastic evidence bag that he'd pulled from his pocket.

I wandered over to the fountain. "I wonder if maybe she was trying to put it in here, to clean it or something."

"I'm pretty sure she has staff for those kinds of things," he said, still looking at the body for any other signs of what might have happened. "Besides, these old fountains aren't made to work with chlorine. It corrodes the system, distorts the natural aging of the stone, and harms any animals who might drink out of it."

"That makes sense," I said, even though I didn't know anything about old fountains and had no clue whether or not it was true. But it did seem to be logical. "Well then, maybe that chlorine tablet is what was used to kill her," I mused.

"Possibly. Do you think it could have been suicide?" he asked.

I thought about it for a second because if there's anything I knew from years of working with rich people, they were often only one bad business deal away from being suicidal. "I'm not sure, but I doubt it. At least not today. I heard she planned all year for this party. It was the one thing she looked forward to."

"Maybe she did it because she knew everyone would be here. Kind of like going out with a bang."

"But then why would she do it *back here* where it was unlikely anyone would find her? It was only by chance that Melinda wandered back here looking for her aunt. Besides, Lady Sinclair also mentioned that Elise didn't like grand entrances," I explained. "So my guess is that she wouldn't have liked grand exits either. Especially not with all of her guests out there. And what about the other set of footprints? You saw them too." The footprints were the most confusing part of this whole thing. Whose could they be?

"True. Given all that, a suicide doesn't really make sense I guess. But without any other evidence, Melinda could

have been the last person to see her. So what are you thinking?" He asked.

"I'm thinking it's too early to draw conclusions but
Melinda is looking really suspicious. She was the one who
found her aunt, which means she could have been the last
one to see her alive. I also took a look at her shoes when
she was standing back here. They look like they match
the shape and size of the second set. And we can't ignore
that she was the heir to the estate." I hated to admit it but
Melinda was looking like the best suspect. I didn't want to
jump to conclusions though.

"When you put it that way..." Sheriff Jackson trailed off,
and kept looking around the body for more clues but came
up with nothing.

Chapter 10

The adrenaline of the situation was starting to wear off and I was getting tired. The forensics team showed up right as I found somewhere to sit and let my nervous system calm down. Guess that would have to wait until later. Sheriff Jackson told them what we'd found and explained that he'd send them the pictures he took of the body before moving it. Of course there was some back and forth about how he should never have moved the body in the first place. He apologized but I could tell it wasn't sincere. He knew moving the body wasn't the right thing to do, but I agreed with his decision. We had to make sure we had the most recent evidence possible. Forensics teams typically did a great job, but there was no substitute for being somewhere shortly after someone died.

Sheriff Jackson waved me over to him, and we started making our way out of the maze. It felt much different now than it had on my way in. There were so many people meandering into the courtyard that we were easily able to follow them and wind our way out. Suddenly some flood lights turned on from way overhead.

The investigators attached them to the trees and it lit up the entire maze. That would have been helpful an hour ago, I thought to myself.

Outside of the maze, the scene was controlled chaos. There were groups of people clustered everywhere. Some congregated around the Shantytown officers who were questioning people. Others were talking in small groups amongst themselves, fueling the local rumor mill. I thought it was a little weird that no one was trying to get their cars from the valet though. They'd been told they couldn't, but I figured there would be at least a few people who would ignore that command. Surely there were some people who intended to show up here, make an appearance and then head to their next event of the evening.

Actually, I'd hoped some people would be trying to get their cars and get out of here early, because whoever the killer was — if there was a killer — they would likely try to get out of here before the cops came. But they also wouldn't want to make a scene. That would give the valet something to remember and tell the police later. So if the potential killer wasn't able to quietly get out, it made sense they'd be mingling with everyone else.

Of course, there was the chance that it was someone who wouldn't be leaving at all. Someone like Melinda. I walked over to the valet, a serious-looking man who appeared to be in his forties.

I noticed his name tag. "Hi, Louis," I tried to sound authoritative but friendly.

"Hello ma'am. I'm sorry but I can't get your car until —" he started to say, but I cut him off.

"Don't worry, I'm not here for my car," I waved away the apology. I was sure that plenty of people had already made him feel stressed out for doing his job and following the sheriff's directions to not let anyone leave. I hoped my tone would put him at ease and make him more likely to talk to me. "I'm helping with the investigation and I was hoping you would be able to answer something for me."

"Oh, uh sure. Whatever you need," he said. My friendly tactic worked.

"I was wondering if you saw anyone leave before you were instructed not to give anyone their keys?" I asked, still trying to keep up a chatty tone.

"Someone leaving before the party?" he asked, taking a minute to think. "Who was it you're looking for? Maybe that'll help me remember better."

"I'm not sure," I admitted, then let the silence sit between us. Typically silence made people uncomfortable and they'd talk to fill it.

"You know, I think I did see a car leave, but I think it was one of the staff," he explained.

"Do you know who it was?" I tried not to sound too hopeful.

"No, I can't say that I do. It was a man in an older brown work truck. He drove up from the staff parking lot and out the front gate. It seemed like he was in a hurry."

"The staff parking lot?" I asked. How big was this place that it had multiple parking areas?

"Yes, there's a separate lot down there." Louis pointed to a small packed dirt road that seemed to go past the far side of the house and sloped down somewhere below it. I'd never noticed it before, but then again, this was my first time here so that wasn't entirely out of the ordinary.

"Did he look familiar to you or do you remember any distinguishing characteristics?" I asked, trying to jog his memory about any little detail his brain may already be forgetting.

"No, but I only work here one day a year, for this party. The only person here I interact with is Leonardo Casa, the house manager," he said, but kept explaining, "I didn't get a great look at the guy. I just saw that he had sort of tan skin and was wearing a black baseball hat and sunglasses. Sorry, I know that's not much to go on."

"That's really helpful. Thank you." I started to walk away, then realized I had another question. "One more thing. Do you know if there are security cameras on that road?" Most wealthy people had tons of security cameras, but Elise was not most people so I couldn't assume that.

Louis confirmed my suspicions and shook his head. "As far as I know there are no cameras anywhere on the premises. Mrs. Huntington-Wilbury valued her privacy, as I'm sure you know. She didn't like the risk someone could hack into them. I tried to talk her into getting them a few times, both to protect her guests and to protect my drivers if they were accused of stealing something. But she wouldn't budge."

"Okay. Thanks again for your time," I said and walked back to where Sheriff Jackson was standing in the yard to see if he'd learned anything. Before I had the chance to get him though, Lady Sinclair spotted me. She started waving her arms and hands, trying to flag me down from the table she was at with Melinda and some other people. She didn't wait for me to walk over to her and instead made a beeline towards me. I couldn't help but notice how graceful she was, even when walking fast in high heels. She really must have been something to behold in her heyday.

I walked at a slower pace to meet her, but while I did that, I looked around the crowd again to see if I could spot anyone looking or acting suspicious. Nothing stood out to me though.

"Tawny, tell me. What have you uncovered so far." Lady Sinclair demanded, a little out of breath.

Chapter 11

I wasn't sure how much I could tell Lady Sinclair, since she had a penchant for gossiping. On one hand, I knew she'd use whatever I told her to draw details from other people. That was how gossiping worked. A person shared a secret and in return was given another secret. But on the other hand, if some of the more sensitive details got out, then that could harm the case.

Deciding to be conservative, I said, "Well not much more than I knew before the sheriff got here," choosing to withhold the tidbit about the chlorine tablets until we got more information about that back from the lab. If that was what killed her, it would be terrible for it to become public knowledge so early in the investigation. I had to give her *something* though or she wouldn't stop asking. "But I did learn that the valet saw one of the staff leaving in a brown work truck."

That piqued her interest. "What?! Who?! When?!" Lady Sinclair exclaimed so loudly that a few heads nearby turned our way. She lowered her voice and put her arm around my shoulder, turning us away from the crowd and off to the side. "Did the valet say who it was?"

"He said he didn't get a good look at the guy. But he had tanned skin and wore a black baseball cap and sunglasses. Apparently he left some time after when guests started arriving and before the body was found. Do you have any idea who it could be?" I hoped that some of those details would jog Lady Sinclair's memory since she probably had been up here more times than anyone else in the town. Surely she'd come across some of the staff. But there was also the chance that this person wasn't staff at all and was merely playing the part to get away with this. Lady Sinclair stayed silent for a few moments, which I had never seen her do before.

Finally she said, "You say he was wearing a black baseball cap and sunglasses? Well, those are quite common things for people to wear, don't you think? They aren't really conclusive about who it could be." Her body language had changed a little, like she didn't want to consider this detail at all and hoped I'd forget it too.

This response made me think that she knew more than she was saying. I couldn't let her know that. I had to make her think she was fooling me if I was going to get her to tell me the truth. "Yes, but anything could be helpful in finding the driver of the truck. Even if you *think* it sort of sounds like someone you know here, it could give us a place to start."

"I suppose you're right," Lady Sinclair was pensive, but then snapped out of it, almost as though she was assuming a different role. "But I wouldn't think too much about it," Lady Sinclair said, standing up straighter, which I'd learned from our sessions she tended to do when she was getting defensive. "There must be other promising leads. Did you find out anything else?"

At this point, I was pretty certain Lady Sinclair was holding something back, but I couldn't figure out what it was. One thing was clear though, and that's that I couldn't fully trust her, which meant I couldn't tell her any other information even if she might be able to shed light on it.

She made it obvious that she was in no mood to clear things up. In fact, if she was hiding something, she may be more likely to lead the investigation astray. So I simply said, "No, that's all for now. How about you?" If she had learned anything, she wouldn't be able to keep it a secret for long, but I'd have to take it with a grain of salt.

"As a matter of fact, I did learn something," she lowered her voice almost to a whisper. "As you know, Elise didn't have many friends but I was among the few she had," she paused, apparently waiting for me to confirm that fact. I nodded and she continued. "We were talking on the phone one day, planning for this tea party when she mentioned her finances were tight, which was a shock to me, as you can imagine."

That shocked me, too. "How odd. Did she say why?" I asked. I was sure this estate took a lot of cash to keep running, but I'd also assumed that Elise had been taking it from various investments or some kind of trust or something. It wouldn't be the first time a wealthy person ran out of money.

"I don't know. I couldn't get the entire story out of her. But she did say she'd have the bulk of her fortune back soon. She said as soon as her lawyers were done exposing some Swiss Ponzi scheme or something. I tried to get more information about it but Elise clammed up. Like she was embarrassed she'd mentioned it at all," Lady Sinclair lowered and shook her head, as if she was sharing in Elise's shame at not having the money.

"A Swiss Ponzi scheme?" I mused, wondering how fast the sheriff would be able to get ahold of Elise's financial records and see if there was any truth to this. I knew there had to be though, because why would someone make up something like that.

"It was quite peculiar. I ended up paying for the catering, and she promised to pay me back," Lady Sinclair sighed, "But I doubt I'll see a dime of that now. Oh well..."

The wheels in my head started turning. "You paid for the catering?"

"That's what I *just* said. Please don't make me repeat myself, Tawny. It's rude," Lady Sinclair huffed.

I ignored her attitude and continued on this train of thought. "So you were here before the guests started arriving? To meet the caterer?"

"Yes. So what?" she crossed her arms, annoyed that she couldn't figure out where I was going with this.

"Then you were here when whoever was driving that truck was here. You *must* have seen him during the preparations. Think a little harder," I urged. But this apparently angered Lady Sinclair who flushed at my accusation. I wasn't sure why. The logic made perfect sense.

"I said I didn't see him. Why are you badgering me about this? If you'll excuse me, I need to go... go..." Lady Sinclair struggled to find the words for where she needed to flit off to next, and it was clear she didn't have anywhere to go. "Well, I just have to go. You know, circulate," she turned and marched away, fitting effortlessly into another crowd of people.

Chapter 12

I looked across the lawn to see that Sheriff Jackson had just finished talking to a couple in matching navy blue ensembles. Actually it seemed like a lot of the couples were in color coordinated attire. I saw Sheriff Jackson wrote a couple more notes in his pocket-size notebook then slipped it in the inner pocket of his jacket.

When he looked up, I was already walking towards him, hoping to sort out these theories before they slipped my mind. I always found that talking through something helped solidify it for me, like how telling someone a dream you had will help you remember it a lot longer than telling no one and forgetting it within minutes.

"Got anything?" Sheriff Jackson asked.

"A few theories, yeah," I nodded, once we were face-to-face, not wanting anyone nearby to be able to hear them.

"That's good," he smiled. "Because I've got almost nothing. What are you thinking?"

"Melinda is an obvious suspect —" I started to say, but Sheriff Jackson held up a hand and cut me off.

"Actually, you know what, I'm just about done here. The investigators will hand in their reports, and no one likes a micromanager," he laughed at his own comment. "So why don't we get out of here. Get some dinner at DINE." It was a statement, not a question.

"You're already done talking to everyone?" I was surprised at how fast they'd worked.

"Between my people and the folks the county sent in to help out, it looks like they'll be releasing everyone to leave soon enough.

And then we'll be stuck in traffic. You want to deal with that?" he asked.

I definitely did not. "No, you've got a point. Okay, DINE it is. I'll meet you there."

"But speaking of cars, how am I going to get the valet to give me mine?" I thought aloud.

"I'll let Louis know to give you your keys," Sheriff Jackson added and walked off.

As I made my way to the valet booth, I looked around and wondered how much longer everyone else would have to stay. Then once I got to the booth, I realized they'd already been letting people go one by one after it was determined whether a person needed to be questioned further or not.

I got to the end of the valet line just in time to see the sheriff hop in his car and drive off. I sighed because the line was longer than I'd anticipated. Then again, I hadn't thought that anyone would be in line at all. I tried to make the most of it, and saw it as a good opportunity to look around again. But this time from a different vantage point.

I hadn't spent much time in the front of the house when I'd arrived, since I was following the flow of human traffic back to the party. It really was incredible, and the way the building was lit up only made it look even more impressive. Then I noticed a few places ahead of me in line stood Duncan Harris, my rival. I hadn't noticed him the entire night but obviously he'd already been questioned and released if he was waiting for his car. I'd heard a rumor that he had trained Elise a few times leading up to her party. My source was of course Lady Sinclair, who had mentioned it because she was trying to persuade Elise to start working with me.

Before I had a chance to finish taking in the scene, Louis pulled up with Ole Reliable, which looked totally out of place amongst the other sports cars and tank-like SUVs surrounding it.

"Wow, that was fast," I said when the valet handed me the keys.

"The sheriff said you had an emergency and needed to leave immediately. I hope everything is okay," he explained, opening my door. As I slid inside the driver seat, I looked up to see I was getting a few eye rolls and dirty looks from people who were still in line. Duncan and I made direct eye contact and as usual, he looked like he absolutely hated my guts. I closed my door and hurriedly drove away.

Chapter 13

There was a little traffic on the winding hillside roads, but it wasn't too bad. I was secretly a little grateful for it because the flow of traffic meant that I didn't have to turn on my phone's GPS to make my way down. That reminded me, I hadn't looked at my phone since I used the flashlight on it in the maze. I took a quick glance and saw that the battery was dead.

When I pulled up to DINE, I could see through the large front window that Sheriff Jackson was already sitting in my favorite corner booth.

DINE was the local diner. If the kitchen was the heart of the home, DINE was the heart of the town. Patrons were almost guaranteed to run into their neighbors every time you set foot in there. It had a 1950s train dining car aesthetic but over the years was upgraded to match the clientele.

The restaurant served all of the standard greasy spoon staples, like burgers and fries but they offered an upscale twist. So instead of a standard burger and fries, you'd get a wagyu burger or a portobello burger and truffle fries. Their milkshakes came in giant glass mugs, adorned with candy and other treats.

These touches gave it a small town feel. But the thing that kept people coming back was its Classic Menu, which offered standard fare. So if you didn't want to pay for the $20 burger, there was a $5 option too, which was a steal. All of the food was locally sourced and classically constructed: just a bun, patty, lettuce, tomato, and onion. Real simple and classic... and affordable. It really was a place where there was something for everyone.

"How'd you know I always sit here?" I asked as I walked back towards him.

"Lucky guess," he laughed. "Kidding. I told Sandi that you were meeting me here and she pointed to this table." He sipped his coffee, which was brewed from a blend of arabica beans specially picked for this specific diner. It was the best coffee I'd ever had.

Before I even had a chance to sit down, DINE's owner Sandi Pritchett walked over to our table with a fresh cup of coffee for me, and she brought the pot with her.

Sandi was one of my first friends in Shantytown. She was in her mid-60s with kind eyes and curly brunette hair that she kept back off her face with a headband. We were similar in that people tended to tell us their secrets, but neither of us was one for gossip. So we *typically* wouldn't pass on the information. Tonight was different though. Someone had died and I knew Sandi likely had information that could help me and Sheriff Jackson figure out what was going on.

"Hey Sandi. Slow night?" I nodded at the dining room that was empty aside from us.

"It always is on the evening of the Huntington-Wilbury party. But I'm sure people will be trailing in here soon. That's why I've got Ferdi here, too!"

The chef, Ferdinand, poked his head out from the kitchen in the back. "Hi, Tawny! Hi, Sheriff!" He flashed his bright smile that looked even brighter thanks to his olive skin. "We're getting ready for the rush!" He announced, then disappeared back into the kitchen.

"A rush, huh?" Sheriff Jackson asked.

"That's right; especially since they obviously didn't get the party that they hoped for," Sandi looked at us as though waiting for one of us to break the dam of information and tell her what happened.

"Good. Then we can ask you a few questions before the crowd gets here," Sheriff Jackson said.

I was glad he stepped in. I knew that *I* trusted Sandi with my secrets, but I wasn't sure if he had the same kind of relationship with her. It appeared that he did though, and I had to admit I was surprised he seemed to be on the same information-sharing level with Sandi.

"Am I under suspicion?" Sandi joked, and I had to suppress a pang of jealousy, wondering if they were flirting with each other. Then I quickly pushed that thought out of my mind, realizing how silly that sounded, both that Sandi would be flirting with someone young enough to be her son *and* that I was acting jealous over a man who I'd barely met a few hours ago.

"Depends. Can you prove you were here all day?" He continued the joke. She simply pointed at her security camera in the corner as she slid into the booth next to me, topping off my cup of coffee.

"You got a warrant?" Sandi said, and we all three chuckled. But it was clearly time to move on from the joke. "So tell me what happened? All I heard is that Ms. Huntington-Wilbury was found dead at the party. That must have been horrible," Sandi said in a low tone, even though there was no one around except for Ferdinand who might overhear our conversation, and he was all the way back in the kitchen.

"Geeze, word really does travel fast here." Since we were some of the first to leave the mansion and there was very little cell phone reception up there, I was surprised Sandi had heard already. Then again, she had deep roots in Shantytown and lots of friends. She probably heard about most things before other people.

"The short version is that Melinda found her aunt lying face down in one of the courtyards of her garden maze. And that's all we really know at this point, aside from some pieces we're trying to put together," Sheriff Jackson explained. I wondered why he didn't say more about what we'd found. Maybe even though Sandi was clearly trustworthy he still didn't want to let out too many details too early in case they leaked. And that leak could obviously be traced back to the two of us.

"So what questions do you have for me?" Sandi asked, and I wondered what angle he was going with.

"Tell me what you know about Melinda," he took another sip of his coffee and I noticed he was very calm. I wondered how he could be so chill when he had a high-profile murder to solve, but maybe that was just his personality, cool under pressure.

"I don't know much," Sandi said. "She's a socialite. I don't think she has a job other than traveling around and posting pictures on social media. She's called an *influencer*," she said "influencer" like it was a word in another language. "Most of what I know about her is only what I've seen in the headlines."

"What kind of headlines?" I asked, unsure what Melinda could do that would get her press.

"Oh, just some stuff that she got into after her dad died. He was very rich, you know?" Sandi asked.

"I'd assume everyone in that family was well-off. What kind of stuff did she get into?" My curiosity was piqued.

"The normal stuff any young, dumb, rich kid gets into. DUI, unflattering pictures of her partying, I think there may have been some drugs but can't remember," Sandi looked off to the side, as though trying to remember more things.

"And she made *national* news?" I asked.

"Sort of but not really. It was mostly just Page Six stuff, and the socialite magazines ran some profile about her after she 'cleaned up her act,'" Sandi put this last part in air quotes. "But, come to think about it, I haven't seen any negative headlines about her since then, so maybe she really did get cleaned up. Now she just travels around the world and keeps quiet, though I bet she wishes she could get a headline or two. It would probably help boost her follower count."

"So it was mostly just a kid acting out? Nothing underground or nefarious?" I pressed.

"No, nothing like that. Why? Do you suspect some foul play?" Sandi asked.

"Not at this time," Sheriff Jackson interjected, cutting me off to stop that story before it had a chance to grow in Sandi's mind.

"But we did find out something interesting, straight from Melinda. Did you know that she is the heir to Ms. Huntington-Wilbury's estate?" I asked.

"No!" Sandi was clearly shocked by the news. "I would have thought Elise's estranged husband would have gotten it all."

"That's what I thought too, but I asked Melinda and apparently they had a prenup," I explained.

"Well, that is interesting, isn't it." Sandi thought for a moment longer, then offered, "You know, Melinda has been spending a lot of time in Switzerland lately, according to her Instagram feed. I wonder if she made some less-than-wholesome friends while she was over there?"

"Did you say Switzerland?" I asked, unable to believe my ears. The coincidence was too perfect.

"Yeah, why?" Sandi looked at me with curiosity. "Do you think that has something to do with Elise's death? I only mentioned it because I couldn't come up with anything else that might be more helpful, but I didn't actually think much of it."

I looked to Sheriff Jackson to see if he cared if I told Sandi. He must have read my mind because he nodded, then sipped his coffee.

I continued on, "Well, keep this to yourself—"

Sandi crossed her heart using her pointer finger, indicating she'd keep the secret.

"I'm not sure, but Lady Sinclair mentioned that Elise had been having money issues because of some Swiss Ponzi scheme she got caught up in recently," I explained. "Her lawyers were looking into it but Lady Sinclair doesn't think they've come to any conclusions yet."

Sandi sat in silence for a moment, thinking. "You know, there was one post where Melinda insinuated that she had a boyfriend. This is very speculative but I wonder if they could have been in on it together?" Sandi offered.

"Possibly, but let's not get too far ahead of ourselves," Sheriff Jackson reigned in the conversation before we started spinning in too many directions.

"You're right. Best not to jump to conclusions yet, so you don't overlook something important. What else have you got?" Sandi asked. "You better hurry up and tell me because once the diners come pouring in, I'll be no use to you anymore."

"One more thing. Do you know what staff Elise had working for her?" I asked. "The sheriff's men will question all of them, of course, but Louis the valet said he spotted a work truck leaving before the party started. He said the driver was someone who was tan, wearing a black baseball hat, and sunglasses. Drove up from the staff parking lot."

Sandi paused and thought for a second. "That doesn't ring any bells, and it's California so everyone is tan. But you know who would know is Lady Sinclair." Sandi leaned in conspiratorially, once again talking just above a whisper as though she didn't even want the walls to know what she was about to say. "You didn't hear it from me, but she had a thing going with the pool boy. I don't know his name but that tidbit of info trickled down to me through the grapevine. I doubt you'll get *her* to admit to it though."

Chapter 14

S heriff Jackson and I exchanged surprised expressions. That would explain why Lady Sinclair was acting so cagey when I brought up the man in the truck. Just then, the bell above the door rang and the navy blue couple I had seen at the party earlier walked in. Sandi hopped to her feet. "I'll check in with you kids later," she said, then topped off both of our coffees and walked over to seat the couple. I took a big inhale of the steam coming off the coffee.

"So it looks like we might have two leads," I said as quietly as I could. The navy blue couple wasn't sitting near us — I had a feeling Sandi did that on purpose — but it would be best if we kept what we knew a secret.

"It seems that way." He paused and took a sip of his coffee. I followed suit. Then he said, "Look, Tawny, I don't want to sound ungrateful, because you really have been a big help so far, but I don't think you should do anything else with this case."

The comment caught me completely off guard. I'd started feeling a camaraderie with him, and not only because I thought he was the best looking man I'd seen in months. For the last few hours we'd had the strongest rapport that I'd ever had with a cop investigating the same incident as me. I couldn't hide my shock. "Are you serious?!" I said in a voice that was definitely louder than a whisper, but I made sure to keep it from being a yell. I knew it was pride getting the best of me, but as a good investigator I could definitely help on this case.

Sheriff Jackson smiled and said, "Gotcha." Then he laughed to himself, sipping his coffee again.

I let out a sigh of relief and smiled, not because I cared that much about helping on the case — although secretly it did feel good to be working on something like this again. I smiled because that kind of reaction from him would have blown up the picture I had in my head of the type of guy he was. But seeing him here, making jokes when anyone else in his position would be stressed with all of the attention this investigation would get made me think his easy-going nature really was who he was and not just a persona he tried to convey.

It made me realize something else: we hadn't discussed whether or not this was an accidental death or a murder. "You had me going there, Sheriff," I laughed. "I have a question for you though. I know you have to wait to get results back from the lab, but what does your gut say this was? Do you think she fell and hit her head or do you think it was a murder?" I asked. I wasn't sure if he'd give me an answer but it was worth asking.

"Well, I think you uncovered some compelling evidence with those disappearing footsteps. I also think there were quite a few people who had reason to kill her. Additionally, her head wound also seemed in an odd place. Why would she be walking backwards towards the fountain!"

I nodded along, but when he didn't continue it became clear to me that he wanted my thoughts on the incident, too. "I agree with all of that," I said. "I'm definitely more inclined to say this was a murder."

The bell over the front door rang again and two more couples came into DINE. Sandi looked up at us to see if we were still discussing. I nodded to her that we were, and she sat them on the other side of the restaurant.

"So do you have any other thoughts you want to share before I get out of here?" Sheriff Jackson asked. He must have been thinking the same thing I was, which was that we were running out of time before this place filled up with partygoers.

"Depends. I'm not sure if I want to tell you now. Maybe I'll keep it to myself and run my own investigation," I tried to make sure he knew it was a joke, but the quizzical look on Sheriff Jackson's face told me that he didn't get it.

"Kidding obviously," I laughed nervously, not sure why I forced such an out-of-character joke just to match the one he'd made earlier. I continued on quickly, hoping he'd forget about it. "I think Sandi was onto something when she mentioned the time Melinda spent in Switzerland. Seems more than coincidental that Melinda was there while a Ponzi scheme was tying up her aunt's money."

"I agree. We need to find out who that boyfriend is. My money is on him playing part in this," he said.

"Do you think he had anything to do with killing her?" I asked.

Sheriff Jackson shook his head. "I don't know yet, but murder or no murder if there was a Ponzi scheme, that's illegal and needs to be prosecuted too," he finished off his coffee in one last gulp. A few more people entered the diner and I could feel their eyes looking at us. But Sheriff Jackson didn't seem like he was ready to go just yet, as he leaned back in his seat. That was just fine with me because I had about a half of a cup left.

"What about this pool boy?" he asked.

"That *is* pretty odd. If I'd known that Lady Sinclair had a thing going on with him while I was talking to her back at the party, then I'd definitely say she was hiding something."

"Do you think *he* did it? And she's helping him cover it up?" he asked. I was used to the police trying to disprove what I thought just to discredit my work, or actively working against me. This was a nice change.

"I don't know the pool guy, but I know Lady Sinclair. I don't think she'd do something like that," I said, but secretly I was doubting everything I knew about Lady Sinclair now.

"You sure? She's an actress after all," he raised his eyebrows.

"I'm sure," I said confidently, even though I was feeling less confident by the minute. "I can't believe she'd do that purely because she couldn't handle keeping it a secret. That alone would kill her," this was something I was confident in. As much as I wasn't sure about Lady Sinclair in general anymore, I was definitely sure about what I'd just said. Carrying a burden like that is something she couldn't possibly sustain. Besides she may have come across as cold, but that didn't make her a murderer. If that were the case, she'd have to be some kind of sociopath.

"You seem like you're questioning your answer," Sheriff Jackson asked, interrupting my thoughts.

"No, just thinking about how shocked I would be if she did have something to do with it," I said with complete honesty.

Just then, Sandi sat a couple down at the table next to ours — the last one available in the diner. This meant we could no longer talk about the case without being overheard

I looked at the rest of the coffee sitting in my cup, but couldn't bring myself to drink it. I had a feeling it was already going to be hard enough to get to sleep tonight.

We scooted out of the booth, Sheriff Jackson walking behind me. I waved to Sandi on the way out, but she was already in the middle of taking someone else's order.

When we got outside to our cars, Sheriff Jackson waved goodbye and said he'd let me know if there were any major developments. I had to admit I was disappointed to see him go. Aside from being easy on the eyes, he was easy on the nerves. There was something soothing about his calm presence which I typically didn't feel in my own life.

Chapter 15

As soon as I got home, I changed out of my tea dress and into some comfy sweats. Then I started the part of my job that I did best: internet sleuthing. In the past, "old school" P.I. work involved a lot of hours on the road, trying to track down leads and conducting stakeouts. But nowadays if someone knew what they were doing, they could spend an hour online and find out more about a person in that time than they previously could in a day or two. As much as I trusted that Sheriff Jackson was good at his job, I had a hunch he wasn't great at social media stalking.

Recalling the information Sandi gave us, I immediately opened Instagram and headed to Melinda's profile to see what I could find there. It appeared she was stuck at the dreaded 200,000 follower mark. It sounded like a lot of followers to most people, and it technically was, but I'd learned from a previous case that this particular figure is a frustrating place for any aspiring influencer. On one hand

200,000 was enough followers to get smaller brands to send you things, but not enough to get the big bucks from major sponsors.

I swiped through a few scrolls of her pictures, careful not to accidentally tap a picture and "like" it. That would send her a notification and be a dead giveaway that I was checking out her profile.

There were lots of pictures of Melinda posing in foreign picturesque places with a generic caption that could apply to any of her other pictures. Things like "Living the good life" and "Wish you were here." I thought it was a little odd that she hadn't posted any from the tea party. But that was likely because most people who spent time curating their image needed to edit the photos first. This meant she didn't post live from events, unless she posted to her Story, and there was nothing there. Story posts disappeared after 24 hours so it didn't matter as much if they were professionally edited.

After about 15 minutes of carefully clicking through her pictures, I saw an image of a charcuterie board filled with Swiss meats and cheeses. A person was tagged in the picture. I tapped to see who it was. @DarioSchmid was the Instagram handle.

I tapped on the name and was taken to his profile. It was private which meant all that I could see was his photo, bio, and follower count. His profile photo looked professional, like something a white collar employee might have and he didn't have many followers which meant he was definitely not an influencer. But at least I had a name I could use to get the search going.

I Googled as much as I could about him. On the first page of the search results there were several links to an investment firm. I clicked on it.

Under the "Who we are" header, there was the same picture of Dario as he'd used in his Instagram profile. He had the title "Associate Economist" written below it. This meant he wasn't a senior person at the firm, and was likely trying to work his way up. If he had concocted some sort of scheme to get Elise's money, maybe it was how he was planning to climb the corporate ladder. It wouldn't be the first time someone did something nefarious to make it look like they were bringing in money to get a promotion. But after clicking around more, this company seemed old and reputable. Then again, most of it was in another language and I was relying on Google's translation tools. So there was a significant chance that something was getting lost in translation.

I went back to the Google search results, looking under Dario's name *and* Melinda's name to see if I could find any events or anything else they'd attended together. Socialites like Melinda tended to show up in the local trade papers when there were charity or black tie events, with theirs and their date's names listed in the caption. But I couldn't find anything else to tie them together besides that one picture.

That must have been what Sandi was talking about when she said that she saw something insinuating Melinda had a boyfriend. But that was *barely* enough to assume that they were actually together. I kept the thought in the back of my mind and decided to call it a night.

I looked at the clock; it was past midnight. I laid down, trying to get some sleep. It wasn't much use though. I partially blamed the coffee I drank so late in the evening. After waking up several times during the night, I decided to give up on sleep and go for a sunrise run.

One of the things I loved about Shantytown was its beach. It wasn't a private beach by any means, but it sometimes felt like it. Despite the seaside mansions being so huge, the scene still somehow pulled off looking quaint. It was almost like some sort of magical filter was over the town that veiled how much money the townspeople actually had.

This particular morning, the weather was overcast and cool, and a thick marine layer created a greenhouse effect. This was my favorite weather to run in. It was crisp but the moisture helped me work up a sweat. I got into a rhythm running on the sidewalk that was adjacent to the beach, and began to mentally go over the plan for the day.

Since the tea party was the night before, my regular clients had all canceled their morning appointments today which gave me some time to keep poking around online. I knew I'd done a thorough search last night, but I also knew my brain had been through a lot of thinking that day. With fresh eyes I might be able to spot something I'd missed.

Then I remembered I hadn't called Jessica to fill her in on everything that had happened. Jessica was the reason I'd been at the party, after all. Slowing to a walk, I pulled out my phone and texted:

TAWNY: Call me when you get a break from filming. Big news. Mad Hatter's dead.

Since Jessica was on set, her hours were all over the place. So, I didn't expect a response back right away and slipped my phone back into my pocket, then I heard it chime, indicating I had a text message. It was from an unknown number, but the mystery of who the sender was ended as soon as I opened it.

UNKNOWN: Tawny, I'm bringing Lady Sinclair in for official questioning. Thought you should know.

Sheriff Jackson. I quickly saved his number before replying.

TAWNY: Thanks for telling me. By the way, how did you get my number?

SHERIFF JACKSON: I have my ways.

TAWNY: Apparently. Why are you questioning Lady Sinclair? Did you find something new?

SHERIFF JACKSON: The autopsy isn't done but the tests are back for that wrapper and for the substance coming out of Ms. Huntington-Wilbury's mouth. Both were chlorine. So we need to know more about that pool boy.

That was an interesting development. I wondered if they'd find that chlorine was the cause of death. I hoped not because that would be a lot more painful than a simple hit to the head.

Since I didn't have any plans for the day, I thought it would be a good opportunity to observe Lady Sinclair. She'd surprised me in the past 24 hours by holding back information for once. I wanted to be on her side but I wasn't sure if I could after she lied to my face about the driver of the car sounding familiar. If I could watch the questioning, then I could see her initial reactions.

TAWNY: Can I come observe?

SHERIFF JACKSON: If you can get here within the next 20 minutes. Already sent an officer to go get her and bring her in.

TAWNY: I'll see you then.

Chapter 16

I hurried home and got ready to go to the Sheriff's Station. After trying on a few outfits, I stopped. Why was I fussing over which outfit I should wear? Normally I didn't put much effort into how I looked at all. As a P.I. you always want to blend in so fashion is never something that was on my radar. Then when I became a personal trainer, I started living in leggings and sports bras.

I blamed this new obsession with my looks on Sheriff Jackson and chastised myself for being concerned about a crush in the middle of an investigation. I settled on what I would normally wear: a pair of black leggings and a white t-shirt. I grabbed my keys and drove out to the station. Thankfully it was only about a five-minute drive, so I got there before the squad car bringing Lady Sinclair did.

I sat in the parking lot for a couple of minutes contemplating what I should do. If I went in now, I could watch the interview and she'd never know I was there... unless she spotted my car, which was a possibility. Or I could wait here and walk in like I happened to arrive at the same time that she had. From what I knew of Lady Sinclair though, she'd see right through that. So I decided to move my car out of sight from where she'd be able to see it, parking it around the side instead of up front. Then I hurried inside.

Sheriff Jackson was standing at the receiving desk and looked surprised to see me.

"You made good time," he said.

"Well, time is of the essence," I quipped.

"Let me get you to the observation room before Lady Sinclair gets here," he moved out from behind the desk and ushered me towards the back of the station.

I was struck by how few people were working. "Are you short staffed today?" I asked.

"Nope. We've got the usual crew. A couple people are in the field at the Huntington-Wilbury estate cleaning some things up, but other than that it's just me and the officer who should be arriving any minute," he held the door to the observation room open for me to walk through. He followed behind and even though it was a small room, I noticed he was standing a little closer to me than necessary. "Can I get you water or anything while you wait?" he asked.

"No, I'm okay thanks," I answered.

"Okay, well then the next time you see me I'll be on the other side of that glass," he nodded at the one-sided mirror and left.

It was perfect timing because as soon as the door shut, I heard voices on the other side. From their tones, I assumed the officer had arrived with Lady Sinclair. Sure enough, as the voices drew closer, I was positive it was Lady Sinclair I was hearing, even though I couldn't make out what she was saying. Then the door to the interrogation room opened and I saw Sheriff Jackson leading her inside.

At the same time, the door to the observation room opened abruptly and an officer I'd never seen before was standing there. He jumped and let out a surprised yelp when he saw me, clearly expecting no one else to be in the dimly lit room.

"I didn't realize that someone was in here," the officer said. Even though there wasn't much light in here, I could tell he was young, probably just out of high school. What he lacked in age, he made up for in height, standing at what I guessed was around 6'3." "Who are *you*?" he asked.

"Hi, I'm Tawny Monroe," I extended my hand to shake his. "I run the fitness studio a few blocks away."

"Officer Craig Futch. What I mean is why are you in *here*, Ms. Monroe?" He clearly had no idea that I had been helping with the investigation.

"I was at the party yesterday and since I used to work as a private investigator, Sheriff Jackson asked for my help on this case," I explained. He still seemed skeptical so I added, "Since it's so high profile, you know?"

At this he nodded his head but still seemed hesitant. "I guess we can use all of the help we can get on this. The insurance company and county people are already calling non-stop." Our conversation was cut off by the voices coming from the interrogation room.

"Thanks for coming down here," Sheriff Jackson said to Lady Sinclair who was sitting across from him. I couldn't help but notice how out of place she looked in that dingy room. She normally had such a regal air about her, but that all seemed to be wiped away under those harsh lights. But she still looked very put together, like she was on the way to an audition or something.

"Well your officer made it sound like I did not have much of a choice," Lady Sinclair huffed. "What's all this about? Should I have a lawyer here?"

"That's up to you," Sheriff Jackson said. "Do you think you need one?"

"No! Of course not. But I'd like to know why you brought me in? It sounds like I'm not a suspect. So do you have one yet?"

"We have some suspicions," he said, keeping his cool demeanor and giving nothing away.

"Well, get on with it then. Why am I here?"

"We think you might be able to help us figure out who may have had a motive to hurt Elise," he said, appealing to her ego. It worked because she straightened up and softened, until he added, "Tell us about your relationship with Scott Summers, Ms. Huntington-Wilbury's pool boy."

So that was his name, Scott Summers. Clearly Sheriff Jackson's people had been busy doing their homework all night. I wondered if they'd already questioned Scott, too. Sheriff Jackson probably would have mentioned it to me though if that was the case. Then again, maybe he wouldn't have. We only met yesterday so it's not like he had a ton of reason to trust me *that* much yet.

Lady Sinclair raised her hand to her chest as though she was offended at the question. "My *what* with *whom*?"

"There is no need to act naive," Sheriff Jackson said, showing the first bit of edge that I'd seen from him. "We're going to question Mr. Summers after you're done here and we're sure he'll tell us what we want to know. But we wanted to give you the dignity of sharing your side of the story first. Now, tell us about your relationship." There was my answer. He started with Lady Sinclair, not Scott.

Maybe he wanted to get as much information as he could before cornering him.

Lady Sinclair sighed and put her head in her hands. "This is humiliating. What's happening here is truly my worst nightmare." She looked at Sheriff Jackson for some kind of reprieve but he sat there stony and silent. Realizing he wasn't going to let her go until he talked, she sighed again and continued. "It was just a casual thing. As you know, I was one of the only friends who Elise allowed to visit her at home. Well, on one of those occasions, I was by the pool while Elise was inside doing god knows what and Scott was cleaning the pool."

"How long ago was this?" Sheriff Jackson interrupted and Lady Sinclair looked annoyed.

"I don't know. Maybe a year ago. It wasn't this summer so it must have been last," she was annoyed. Then she kept going, not giving Sheriff Jackson a chance to ask any other questions. "We caught each other's eye during one of my visits and flirted. Nothing serious," she paused and it sounded like there was more to the story, but when she didn't keep going, Sheriff Jackson jumped in.

"That's it? All you two did was flirt for over a year?" His tone was flat, not accusatory.

Lady Sinclair blushed and I realized I'd never seen her do that before. "You nosey man! I don't believe that's any of your business!" she cried. Sheriff Jackson was good at interrogation though, and he employed my favorite tool: silence. He just sat there, which caused Lady Sinclair to squirm and get uncomfortable. It was even uncomfortable to watch! Finally she said, "If you *must* know, on subsequent visits, we became more... intimate. But we were very careful to make sure Elise never knew *nor anyone else*," she hastily added the last part adding emphasis implying that he should keep the secret, too.

"Why would it matter if Ms. Huntington-Wilbury knew? You two were friends, so wouldn't that be something friends would discuss?" he asked.

"For my part, I didn't care if Elise knew. I just didn't want it to get out that I was sleeping with the help. It would tarnish my reputation," she straightened her posture, as though subconsciously trying to look more dignified.

"When you say 'for my part' are you insinuating that Mr. Summers also didn't want Ms. Huntington-Wilbury to know about you two?" he asked.

Lady Sinclair exhaled a frustrated sigh. "Must I spell out *everything* for you, Sheriff? Yes, that's what I mean. He mentioned a few times that he might lose his job if she found out."

"Why would that be?" he asked.

"Who knows. I loved Elise. She was a dear friend of mine, but even I can admit that she had a tendency to be eccentric. She could be mercurial, finding one thing or another to fight about when it suited her. I can't even imagine what a nightmare she would be as an employer. She must have fired all of her staff at least two times each," she waved off the question.

"And you're sure that your relationship with Mr. Summers wasn't serious?" he looked a little more at ease now that Lady Sinclair seemed to be opening up.

"I'm perfectly certain," she said, lifting her chin.

"Then why did you try to hide knowing him when Tawny asked you about him driving the work truck?" This was the question that I had been wondering as well.

"Isn't it obvious by now? Because I'd hoped to avoid all of *this*," she said, gesturing at the interview room. "I like my private business to stay private." I thought that comment was ironic coming from her, knowing that when she found out a morsel of gossip, it spread through the town like wildfire.

Sheriff Jackson wrote down a few notes on his pocket notebook but said nothing. I could see the silence was making Lady Sinclair uncomfortable again.

"So, can I go now? Lady Sinclair finally asked, impatient.

"Not quite. Give me a minute," he stood up and left the room, seconds later opening the door to the observation room.

Chapter 17

Sheriff Jackson joined Officer Futch and me. "What do you think?" he asked us.

"Seems like she's telling the truth," Officer Futch suggested. I could tell he was trying to assert authority over the situation by answering before I could.

"I agree," I added. "But I think you should tell her about the chlorine. If she thinks there was a chance *she* was in danger or that Scott killed her friend, then she might be more open to talking. Right now it seems like she thinks her fling was harmless, but she could have been in trouble if it turns out Elise was poisoned." Sheriff Jackson was nodding along but Futch still looked a little confused. "If we make her realize that she was potentially with a killer then she might be more likely to talk," I said plainly for the benefit of Futch.

Sheriff Jackson thought for a second then said, "That's a good idea. But you know what? I think you should be the one to tell her."

"Are you sure?" I was taken aback. I didn't even want Lady Sinclair to know that I was here, let alone question her.

"Yeah, Sheriff. She's not trained in interrogation. Maybe I should ask her," Futch sounded defensive and puffed out his chest a little bit.

Sheriff Jackson ignored Futch and said, "Yes, I'm sure. You already have a rapport with her, Tawny. If you play it right, I think she'll see it as a friend looking out for her when you break the news," he said in his cool, flat tone.

"Well, I'll give it a try," I said and made my way to the interrogation room.

As soon as I walked through the heavy metal door of the room, Lady Sinclair looked up with both surprise and horror in her eyes. "Tawny?! What are you doing here? Oh god, did you hear everything I said? My worst nightmare has come to pass," she cried out, theatrically extending her hands upwards and then lowering them to put her head in her hands. "It's only a matter of time until *everyone* knows, isn't it?" she sighed.

I sat down across from her and tried to sound as friendly as possible. "Yes, I heard it all but don't worry, I won't tell anyone. Besides, you know I'm helping with the investigation. That's all this is," I tried to reassure her. Of course I had a feeling that people would find out sooner or later though. This was a small town and news had a way of getting out. For all I knew, Lady Sinclair herself would be the one to accidentally blab about this to someone to try and get ahead of the gossip.

"Oh, yes, yes of course. All this just has me so flustered," she said, straightening herself and sitting back up. "So why are *you* here now to question me? What else can I possibly say? You know I want to help however I can, I just don't see how *my private life* is of any use." She whispered "my private life" as though there were someone else in the room with us and she didn't want them to hear.

"Well, there's something else you should know. Remember when I was looking at Elise's body for clues while you walked Melinda out of the maze? I found something. It was a plastic wrapper for some kind of tablet. And there was a foaming substance coming out of Elise's mouth," I said but Lady Sinclair held up her hands, indicating to me to stop.

"Oh my God, Tawny, must you be so *graphic*?!" she said, but I knew it was for show. She always wanted as many details about something as she could get.

"Sorry," I said, though I didn't mean it. "Anyways, the test came back for the wrapper already," I paused to try and read if Lady Sinclair's body language would give anything away. She leaned in closer, eager to hear what I would say next. "It tested positive for chlorine."

Lady Sinclair gasped and put her hand to her chest. "No! You don't think she took the chlorine tablet and killed herself, do you?"

I was afraid she was missing the point here and tried to reframe it. "We're still waiting to hear what the official cause of death was, but it's unlikely it was a suicide because of the other footprints in the area." I couldn't tell if her shock was genuine or if Lady Sinclair was giving the performance of a lifetime. "In my opinion, it's more likely that someone forced her to take the tablet and she hit her head falling *after* she'd been poisoned."

"You said it was a chlorine tablet? You can't possibly think that Scott..." Lady Sinclair trailed off, finally putting the pieces together.

"Well you have to admit it's suspicious the valet saw someone who looked like him driving away shortly *after* when she would have been killed and *before* the party started. And then when I asked you about it at the party, you, Elise's best friend lied about not knowing who could be driving the car." I was hoping that this would provoke her into telling me more, but was not quite enough to make her dislike me. After all, she was one of my best clients. I wanted her to feel like we were in on this together. "I'm just saying it looks odd," I was careful not to use the word "suspicious" and put her on edge.

"I don't like what you're insinuating!" she shouted and slapped her hand on the table.

"I'm not insinuating anything, Lady Sinclair. I'm just telling you what happened. You're a smart woman. Surely you can see how those pieces I laid out fit together, can't you?" I said calmly, hoping that by appealing to her ego she'd come back around to being on my side.

It worked. She lowered her voice and said, "I already explained why I didn't admit that I knew Scott. It was only because I was embarrassed and didn't want the word to get out. Especially not at a party where all of the town's most influential people were there. Surely you can understand that, can't you?"

"I get it. And I believe you. But you can see how things look, right? Not to mention you were one of the only guests who was there before the party started. So all that I'm asking you to do is to help me understand. Was the last time you saw Scott before the party?" I hoped Lady Sinclair was now realizing I'd get to the truth one way or another so she might as well just tell me whatever she knew.

Lady Sinclair spoke in a low, defeated tone. "Yes. We were together before the party."

"What did you talk about? Did he seem any different than usual?" I wanted to hurry and get my questions answered while Lady Sinclair was finally in this rare, vulnerable state of mind.

It backfired though and Lady Sinclair was quick to get defensive again. "As I'm sure you've gathered, there generally wasn't much talking between us. But now that you mention it, I guess Scott did seem a little more paranoid about being caught than usual."

"What do you mean?" I asked.

"Usually it was mostly me who was worried about someone seeing us, but this time he seemed worried. He kept checking to make sure no one was spying on us. I just assumed it had to do with the fact that there were more people around, setting up for the party," Lady Sinclair explained.

"I'm sorry to ask this, but where did you choose to, uh, meet up?" I used air quotes around "meetup."

"The pool house, as usual," she said, resigned.

"Where the pool chemicals are kept?" I asked.

"Yes," Lady Sinclair sighed. "Where the chemicals are."

"I'm sorry to have to ask this, too, but now that I know you were in the pool house with Scott before Elise died, you know that you could be a suspect, right?" I asked as delicately as possibly.

"Well... no. I guess I hadn't thought of that," she said quietly. "Is that your question or was there another coming?"

"I'm going to ask you again, is shame the only reason why you pretended not to know who Scott was when I asked you about him driving the truck at the party?" I tried to sound as empathetic as possible.

It worked because she reached across the table and took my hands. "Tawny, I don't know how much clearer I can make this. It was pure ego. I didn't want people to know."

It was probably the most sincere I'd ever seen her in the few months that we'd known each other, but it worked. I was back on Team Lady Sinclair.

I smiled and said, "I believe you, Lady Sinclair. Thanks for doing this; I know it wasn't easy."

"My dear, you don't know the half of it. So am I free to go?" She started to stand.

"I think so. The sheriff will come back in and let you know," I opened the door and Sheriff Jackson was already standing on the other side. He popped his head into the opening of the door and said, "Thanks, Lady Sinclair. Officer Futch is in the car waiting to get you home. Do me a couple of favors though?" Sheriff Jackson asked. Lady Sinclair simply nodded in response. "Don't leave town for a few days and don't contact Mr. Summers. If he contacts you, call me."

"I can do that," Lady Sinclair said, gathering herself and regaining her proud posture. "Good bye, Tawny, Sheriff Jackson," she nodded at each of us and then walked out of the station.

Chapter 18

After she left, I walked back into the main part of the station and noticed that a few more officers arrived while I was in the interrogation room. They were sitting at the computers, tapping away.

"You did good in there," Sheriff Jackson said. "Have you ever considered joining us here at the station? I'm sure you could use your *big city* experience and teach us all a thing or two."

"No thanks. But I'll take the compliment. So who are you talking to next? Is Scott really on his way in right now?"

"Well, since we're still trying to figure out who Melinda's boyfriend is, and we've got that confirmed chlorine on the wrapper, Scott is currently our best lead," he answered.

"Oh! I forgot to tell you. I figured out his name!" I announced, pulling out my phone to show him.

"Whose name? The boyfriend?" He raised his eyebrows in surprise.

I nodded. "His name is Dario Schmid. He works at a Swiss investment firm," I showed him the website for the investment firm but as I did, an alert popped up announcing that Jessica was calling me back.

"How did you figure that out?" he asked.

I waved the question away and said, "I'll tell you later. I have to take this," and quickly walked outside. By the time I was able to answer it, the call had gone to voicemail. I called her back immediately and she answered.

"Jess! How's filming?"

"Filming is fine, but you're crazy if you think *that's* what we're going to talk about! What happened to Mad Hatter? You have to tell me everything!" Jessica was practically yelling into the phone.

I filled her in on everything that happened. Getting to the party and immediately seeing Melinda running out of the maze, and about Melinda's boyfriend Dario, and Lady Sinclair roping me into helping with the investigation. Then I told her about the interrogation we'd just had and the romantic bombshell.

I felt a little bad about betraying Lady Sinclair's confidence, but it was a huge piece to the puzzle, and I knew Jessica would keep it between us. "So what do you think?" I asked once I finished telling her everything.

"Um wow. That's a lot. Well, I have quite a few thoughts! Obviously!" Jessica was still practically yelling. "Just to be clear, my enthusiasm isn't about the death. I just love a mystery."

"I know, it's morbid, but it is what it is," I sympathized. "So tell me what you're thinking."

"Off the top of my head, I'd say look into Melinda and her boyfriend. Obviously, right? It sounds like she had motive *and* opportunity. I'd imagine that's a huge fortune for someone to inherit," Jessica explained, and I had to admit it made the most sense right now.

"But what about the chlorine? That clearly points to Scott, doesn't it?" I was surprised she didn't anchor on what I thought was the more obvious of the two choices.

"It couldn't be *that* hard to go get those tablets and then frame a member of the staff. Besides, what's Scott's motive other than she maybe fired him once?" Jessica reasoned and I had to agree those were some solid points. "But give me more time to think about it," she added.

Just then, I saw Officer Futch pulling back into the station. This time he had Scott in his back seat. As much as I wanted to keep talking with Jessica, I knew I had to get into the observation room to see them question him.

"Jess, Scott just got here. I've got to go," I hurried to get off the phone.

"Oh my gosh! Yes! Go! I'll call you later," Jessica said and hung up.

Chapter 19

I waited for Futch and Scott to go inside then made my way inside too. I couldn't be sure if Scott was lingering near the receiving desk or if he'd made his way into the interrogation room already, so I poked my head around the front door. When I didn't see him, I walked back to the observation room and let myself in.

Officer Futch and Sheriff Jackson were both in there with Scott. Unfortunately the questioning didn't last long because I'd got there right in time to see him ask for a lawyer. Sheriff Jackson and Officer Futch just sat there, employing the silent tactic.

I took a long look at Scott from the other side of the one-way mirror. He looked like a surfer who had stepped right out of a competition. He was tan and clearly fit, with wavy chin-length hair that was bleached blonde by the sun. The coastal waters here were bitterly cold year-round, but it was consistently a great spot for surfing. Scott's voice broke into my thoughts. "I've seen cop shows on TV, man.

I know how this works. You're going to trick me into saying something that I didn't do. I said I want a lawyer," Scott demanded again.

Finally, Sheriff Jackson gave up on the quiet game and left the room. He opened the door to the observation room and looked surprised to see me in there.

"I snuck in when you were already with Scott," I explained before he had a chance to ask.

"It's never a good look when someone asks for a lawyer," Sheriff Jackson noted.

I nodded in agreement. Though there were the rare cases when someone was innocent and just wanted to make sure they didn't get talked into admitting anything by some tricky interrogators. "What are you going to do now?" I asked.

He sighed. "Well it'll be a while before the public defender can get here. He doesn't have a personal lawyer. So I guess I'll just put him in the holding tank until then," he said with a shrug. "There's always the chance he'll crack before the lawyer arrives and want to talk in order to try and get out of here. But first, I'll leave him in there for a while," he pointed to the interrogation room.

"Any idea when you can track down Dario Schmid?" I asked. It felt like a ton of time had passed, but I had to remind myself it hadn't even been 24 hours since we found Ms. Huntington-Wilbury.

"I've got the team working on it," he explained. I looked towards the one person in the office sitting at a computer. This could take awhile. He continued, "In the meantime we'll bring Melinda in for questioning next. If Dario really is her boyfriend, then she's gotta have some idea where he is," Sheriff Jackson reasoned.

I mulled it over quickly. "You and your people haven't found anyone who saw him at the party?"

"Nope. Which is odd in general, but especially if he killed her. Some member of the house staff would have spotted him, I'm sure. So we'll just have to see what shakes out when questioning Melinda," Sheriff Jackson shrugged. Just then, Officer Futch knocked and came into the room. It was pretty cramped with the three of us in there. I didn't mind the proximity to Sheriff Jackson, but Futch looked very uncomfortable to be in such close quarters.

"Sheriff, the coroner is on the phone. They've got the results of the autopsy," Futch explained.

"Wow! That was really fast." I had never heard of an autopsy coming back within one business day of a murder.

"That's what happens when one of the county's wealthiest members was potentially murdered," Sheriff Jackson said.

"I guess so," I added, but was still a little in shock at how quickly that happened.

"I'll be right back, Tawny" he said and left me in the room with Futch trailing behind him. He was crazy if he thought I was going to stay there alone and miss out on the scoop. So I followed suit and trailed them both to the receiving desk where he took the call. I looked on, trying to read Sheriff Jackson's mannerisms. Like always, he was calm and cool, giving away nothing.

"Okay, thanks for the info," Sheriff Jackson hung up. "Well the cause of death is a severe head injury. It is consistent with her hitting it in a fall. She wasn't struck with anything, which is what we suspected. But the odd part is that the chlorine was only on her mouth, not in her stomach or blood," he explained.

That sounded bizarre. "Wait, so she never ingested it?"

"Nope; apparently not," he shrugged.

"So that means she wasn't poisoned, it only *looks* like she was?" I asked, trying to put the pieces together. "But that doesn't make any sense. Who would want it to look like an accidental death and also a poisoning?"

"Someone who doesn't know what they're doing or who knows the fall wasn't an accident," Sheriff Jackson answered. Then he stayed quiet, clearly still mulling over this new development as well.

"If Dario, Melinda, and Scott are still our main suspects, this doesn't change anything, does it?" I asked.

"No, I supposed it doesn't. All of those people presumably aren't experienced killers," Sheriff Jackson responded.

Then Officer Futch interjected, "You never know, Sheriff. I've heard some stories on those late night TV cop shows where the last person you expected is the one who committed the crime." He looked proud about his addition to the discussion.

"It's a good point, Futch. Let's just take it as a sign not to jump to any conclusions. Since Scott isn't talking and we can't question him further, we might as well bring in Melinda," he said. "Futch, do you think you could go —"

I cut in. "Actually, why don't I go visit her at the Huntington-Wilbury estate? If it seems like I'm casually dropping in to chat then she might be more forthcoming."

"You don't think Futch or I should come too?" Sheriff Jackson raised an eyebrow.

"No. That won't seem casual at all. Right now she probably already assumes she's a suspect. You don't want to confirm that for her or she'll clam right up," I explained, but he seemed unmoved. "I'll record the whole thing on my phone, but I won't let her know I'm recording. Unfortunately that means whatever I uncover can't be used in court. It could give us a lead though."

Sheriff Jackson thought it over for a few seconds before saying, "I don't love the idea but it's not a bad plan. And I don't have anything better coming to mind at the moment. You'll let me hear the entire recording once you leave?"

"I don't see why not." I was a little taken aback at his insinuation that I'd hide something from him. It wasn't like anyone was paying me to help out on this case. I was doing it because it was the right thing to do. Besides, I thought it was better than just "not a bad plan;" it was a *good* plan.

"Then have at it. See what you can find," he said.

"Great, I'll call you when I leave the estate," I said and left the station. Little did he know I'd already decided to go ahead with my plan with or without his blessing. This certainly made it easier though.

Chapter 20

I got into my car which was getting more miles in the last two days than it probably had in the last two weeks combined. Before driving up the hill, I searched the map history on my phone and found the address from the tea party. This time I made sure to take a screenshot of the directions in case I lost reception again. Without a party, there wouldn't be a trail of cars I could follow up the hill to guide me if my phone froze. As I hit the button to start giving me directions, I was overwhelmed with an eerie feeling. At this time yesterday, a woman was dying in the house I was currently en route to. Actually, she was probably dying while I was on my way up the hill yesterday, too.

Halfway up to the house, it dawned on me that I wasn't even sure if Melinda would be there or not when I arrived. I didn't have her number so I couldn't call and check. I'd just assumed that after yesterday she'd be at home, grieving and settling her aunt's affairs. After all, when someone dies, there are always so many details to work out.

As I pulled up the winding driveway again, I was pleased to see that my gamble had paid off. Sure enough, the large flat concrete pad at the top of the driveway was as full of vehicles today as it had been yesterday, but this time the vehicles were trucks. It looked like they were hauling away the furniture that had been rented for the party.

I parked my car and got out, surveying the area. It was just as grand as I'd remembered. The front door was wide open, with people going in and out, carrying tables, chairs, and catering dishes. They were probably supposed to take them all away last night, but the investigation foiled any chance of that happening.

Then all of a sudden, a white dog with auburn patches came bursting out of the front door barreling right towards me. It never slowed, running full speed and closing the space between me and him, which was probably about 100 yards. It looked friendly enough, but as it drew closer I was starting to wonder if it saw me as an intruder.

I didn't have to worry for long because the dog abruptly stopped right when it got to me and started rubbing its head on my leg. I'd never seen a dog that looked quite like this one.

It was a little taller than my knee-level with short hair, a mostly auburn head with floppy ears, white body, and spots that matched. I reached my hand down to show it that I was friendly and the dog licked it in agreement.

There was a yell from somewhere in the house. "Muffy! Muffy where are you?!" A middle-aged man dressed in a black suit stumbled out of the doorway. He looked in my direction and said, "Muffy! There you are. Get back here this instant!"

"I guess your name is Muffy, huh?" I said to the dog and I could have sworn she nodded in agreement before bounding back towards the man who made his way to the halfway point between me and the door. Instead of slowing down, Muffy blew right past him and into the house. He stopped walking and let out a sigh so heavy that it was nearly visible. Then he inhaled and straightened himself up again, looking at me. "Can I help you?" he huffed, annoyed by the entire situation.

I waved and walked towards him trying to be as cheerful as was appropriate. I hoped that he wasn't some kind of gatekeeper who could bar me from getting inside the house. As I approached him I said, "Hi, I'm Tawny Monroe. I was here last night helping with the investigation." He looked unmoved. "I'm friends with Melinda and I wanted to drop by to check on her." It was a lie, but I had a feeling that he wouldn't know that. I didn't get the impression that Melinda had been here that often, let alone brought friends to the mansion.

The man straightened out his suit and extended his hand to shake mine. "Hello Ms. Monroe. I'm Leonardo Casa, the house manager," he said with an air of pride. "Ms. Melinda is in the drawing room, off to the right when you walk in. I believe she's talking with someone right now, but if you're a friend she won't mind. I trust you can find your own way. If you'll excuse me, I need to help these people load their vans." Leonardo did a little bow and walked away towards the vehicles that were slowly being filled with stacks of tables.

I walked up to the front door, which was wide open from the people going in and out, and was immediately stunned by the foyer. It was all white marble with what had to be a 30-foot ceiling and a gorgeous crystal chandelier dangling from the ceiling. There were two grand spiral staircases leading up to the second floor which overlooked the entrance where I was standing. I was so blown away that I couldn't even move.

"Tawny? Is that you?" I heard a voice coming from my right and remembered that's where Leonardo said Melinda would be. I looked over and there she was, sitting in yet another grand looking room.

This one had the same royal-esque decor as the rest of the house, with a few couches and lounges scattered throughout and giant bookcases lining either side of the room. It was kind of confusing as to whether it was a study or a lounge. Melinda was sitting at the far end, near a window that was as tall as the entire room. She was talking with another man I'd never seen before. He looked to be in his '50s with a full head of salt and pepper hair, and appeared to be dressed in work clothes. He was sitting next to Melinda and there was an air of familiarity, but not intimacy. I guessed he was just another member of "the staff."

"Melinda! Just the person I was looking for." I tried to sound friendly but was afraid it came off over-the-top. She smiled and waved me over.

"That will be all, Frank. Thank you," Melinda said, and the man rose, gave a slight bow, then left the room.

"Tawny, what are you doing here?" She asked, and seemed happy to see me, which immediately made me feel guilty.

I was curious about who that man was so I decided to try and find out. "I wanted to stop by and see how you were doing but I didn't have your number. I figured it would be easier to just come over here," I tried to sound sincere. "But if you're busy, I can come back later," I motioned towards

Frank who was still walking the long distance back to the foyer.

"Oh no. It's fine. That's just Frank O'Toole, the handyman. There's always something that needs fixing at this old place," she explained.

That's when the realization hit me that all of the people I'd seen so far who worked at this house were men.

"Thank you for coming!" Melinda exclaimed. "Why don't you come sit with me?"

Melinda motioned for me to sit on the opposite end of the couch that she was also sitting on. It was longer than a loveseat but not so long that we had to speak loudly to hear one another.

"Thank you," I sat down and was surprised at how firm the couch was, like no one had ever sat on it before. "So how are you? I mean, how are you *really* doing? Still in shock, I'm sure," I offered, trying to get the conversation going.

"Oh, you know," Melinda theatrically sighed. "There have been people in and out of here all day. Investigators, house staff, party vendors picking up the rental equipment. It's like a revolving door. I haven't had a moment to just breathe."

"That sounds really stressful," I tried to appear sympathetic, but it wasn't lost on me that Melinda hadn't even mentioned her aunt one time yet. It was possible she was in the denial stage of grieving, but I decided to try and broach it anyway. If she truly wasn't sad, then that could point to an indication of guilt. "What about your aunt? How are you holding up with her being gone?"

At this, Melinda pulled back her dramatic flair a bit and leaned in towards me. "If I'm being honest, not well. It was such a shock. The whole thing, you know?"

"I can't even imagine," I offered. Then I realized that I'd been so in awe of this place, I'd completely forgotten to pull out my phone and start recording. That was the entire reason I'd come up here in the first place!

Thinking on my feet, I startled a little, pretended my phone was buzzing in the side pocket on my leggings. "Oh! Sorry, one second. I have a text. It might be my afternoon client," I lied, knowing I didn't have any appointments that day nor had anyone texted me, but Melinda didn't know that. I opened the voice recording app and hit *Record*. Then I locked the screen and put the phone facedown on the table. "Nope, not a client. Just a spam text," I explained, hoping Melinda bought it.

She did. "I get those all of the time, Sooo annoying. Or those scams calling non-stop about extended car warranties. I don't even have a car!" Melinda threw her hands in the air.

"I know, right?" I agreed, continuing to try and build rapport.

"Or I didn't until yesterday. Now I guess I have quite a few. Anyways, where was I? Oh, right, Aunt Elise. I'm sure I'll need therapy to get over finding her like that," Melinda got a little choked up. "I can't even think about it or I'll cry."

"Well you certainly don't have to talk about it if you don't want to. I just wanted you to know I'm here if you do," I tried to reassure her. "But you know, sometimes it helps to get it off your chest. Do you want to talk about what led you to go looking for her?"

Melinda laughed. "I was looking for her because no one could find her! I'd arrived a little early like always and asked where Auntie was. Everyone said they hadn't seen her in awhile. I knew she liked to go in the maze to think or just get away. We always used to walk through there when I was little." She paused, her breath catching for a moment. "So, I figured since everywhere else had been checked, I might as well try the maze."

"I'm so sorry you had to go through that," I said, but I still wanted more information. "Where were you before the party? Don't you normally stay here?"

Melinda waved off the comment. "Not during the days leading up to the party. It's too chaotic."

"That makes sense." I looked around at all of the activity inside and outside the mansion. "It seems like you're mostly surrounded by staff now instead of friends." Over the years I'd learned that people who worked to keep these giant households going were frequently referred to as "staff" and I hoped using this label would make Melinda trust me more, make her think that I understood the world Melinda came from and could relate with her. It worked.

Melinda smiled and said, "Tawny, you see right through me, don't you? All day I've been yearning for a friendly face but I've been met with one task or set of questions after another. You're the first one today to ask me how I was doing. Even though I only met you last night I feel like I can trust you," Melinda said.

I smiled and nodded but cringed inside knowing my motive for being here was anything but friendly. But maybe it could help get her off the hook, depending on what I found out.

"There's something to be said for a kinship being built out of a trauma. You know, since you were there with me after I found —" This time Melinda broke out into tears over the unspoken reference to her aunt. I seized the opportunity to ask some questions while her guard was down.

"I totally agree," I said, feeling sick as the words left my mouth, knowing I was trying to pump this grieving woman for information. "I'm glad I was there at that moment." I was about to mention that otherwise the authorities might have overlooked the second set of footprints since they had mostly disappeared by the time Sheriff Jackson got there, but something told me that pressing her right now wasn't the best way to go about this. "Let's talk about something happier," I offered.

"Oh yes, please, let's," Melinda agreed, wiping a few remaining tears from her eyes.

"I have something to admit. Since I'd just met you last night, I looked around on Instagram and found your profile. I hope that's not too creepy," I added. But I had a feeling Melinda would be flattered by my efforts. "I just felt so bad for you and wanted to get to know you a little better."

"That's not creepy at all!" she gushed, confirming my hunch. "It seems like a totally normal thing to do these days."

"You live quite the glamorous life, don't you? It would make anyone jealous." I hoped that open-ended statements would get her talking as opposed to me firing questions at her.

"Well, it's not all *that* glamorous," Melinda said. "Actually if I'm being quite honest it gets a little lonely at times. I'm not sure if you noticed but nearly all of the pictures are of just me. Sometimes that makes me wonder if it looks a little pathetic."

I had noticed they were mostly of her, but instead of acknowledging it, I lied. "I hadn't noticed at all." I had to admit, I saw a bit of myself in Melinda when I was scrolling through her profile last night. I'd always been a bit of a lone wolf. Maybe that's why I felt myself warming to her even though we couldn't have had less in common and she might be a murderer. I continued trying to keep the conversation moving. "In fact I noticed you tagged a man on a picture of a delicious-looking charcuterie board. Is that your —"

"My my, you really *did* go creeping, didn't you?" Melinda laughed, showing that she wasn't put off by it. "Yes, that's my boyfriend Dario Schmid. He's such a dream." She looked like a smitten school girl when she said it.

"You have to tell me more," I prodded even though it didn't seem like Melinda needed it. I hoped this was about to answer a lot of questions in the investigation.

"We met while I was traveling in Switzerland. I was with a group of international bloggers at the time, and I lost my wallet. I called Auntie Elise to wire me some money —"

At the mention of her aunt, Melinda started to tear up. I was worried she'd start crying and get distracted from the story. Thankfully, she took a deep breath and continued on. "Anyway Auntie Elise wired me $25,000 to get by for a week."

It took every bit of my willpower not to roll my eyes at $25,000 only being enough for a week but I resisted.

Melinda continued. "Since it was a significant sum of money, I had to work directly with a banker to get it wired over. That banker turned out to be Dario. After we got everything settled, he offered to take me to lunch since the funds wouldn't be available for a few hours. And the rest is history."

"He sounds like a real gentleman," I kept using my open-ended statements so she could carry on. This guy sounded nice so far, but there had to be more to the story.

"Oh, he is. In fact, he took such good care of me that I was able to stretch that $25,000 to last for two weeks instead of one. I hardly ever had to pay for a meal out," she said with a little air of triumph.

I suppressed another eyeroll. "Did he ever get the chance to meet your aunt?" I asked.

"Funny you mention that. He was actually supposed to meet her for the first time at the party last night but his flight was delayed and he couldn't make it," Melinda explained.

That made my internal radar go off. A delayed flight was a good cover for someone who was actually around but wanted to seem like he wasn't.

"That's unfortunate timing. So where is he now? Still on his way here, I'm sure," I said.

"He'll be here tomorrow. The flight delay caused a whole *thing* with scheduling and he wasn't able to fly out until today," Melinda explained.

"That's some bad luck. Sorry to hear it," I made a mental note to check on plane schedules and make sure he really was on the flight. Then I realized I didn't know what flight to check on. "Where did you say he was flying out of?"

"His first flight was out of Geneva and that one was fine. It was when he got to New York that he was delayed," Melinda explained. "There were no direct flights available so he had a layover, which turned out to be the longest layover ever."

I remembered hearing about a freak storm along the east coast on the news and began to believe her story a little. If Dario hadn't been at the party then there was no way that he could have been involved at the moment the murder occurred. There was still a chance he got Melinda wrapped up in it though, and that she'd killed her aunt either by accident or on purpose to get the inheritance.

But seeing Melinda sitting here, so insecure and fragile, I had a hard time believing that was the case. I had only met her yesterday though, so I couldn't be positive and reminded myself to keep an open mind.

"That's too bad he never got to meet your aunt," I said hastily, realizing it was taking me longer than was polite to respond. "I never got the chance to meet her either. She seemed like a really lovely lady from everything I heard." That was another lie. Most things I'd heard about her were just facts, not good nor bad.

"Yes, well things like that happen sometimes don't they," Melinda said with the sniffle.

Then something dawned on me. "Are you planning to have a memorial ceremony?" I asked, trying to keep the conversation going, without it veering into territory that would make her cry again. Usually when people were set to get a big inheritance, they were in a rush to get through all of the formalities when the benefactor died. That was especially true if the beneficiary was guilty. Getting everything done faster meant getting to the money faster. If Melinda was guilty, she'd have already started plans for either the memorial or the funeral.

"We'll have a proper funeral once the police release the body, but nothing else for now."

No rush for a memorial snuffed out the cash grab idea for now, but then I was struck with another one. "Hey, if the funeral is a ways off, why don't you have a memorial for her in the meantime?" I asked. "The house is all primed for a party anyway. All you'd have to do is get those tables and chairs off the trucks before they drive away. Think of it like a party in her honor." I hoped the suggestion wouldn't come off as too crass especially since I had an ulterior motive. In my experience, funerals were a great place to spot a killer. If Melinda wasn't guilty, there was a good chance that whoever was would show up to pay their respects to pick up tidbits about where the police were at with their investigation.

I was thankful to see Melinda perk up in her seat, a sparkle in her eye. "Tawny! That is the idea of the *century*, do you know that?" She exclaimed, standing up in the lounge and clapping her hands. Then she cupped her hands around her mouth and shouted, "Everyone who can hear my voice, stop what you're doing! Put everything back!"

All of the background sounds of people moving things instantly quieted. I hadn't realized how noisy it had actually been until that moment when it was nearly silent.

Chapter 21

Melinda sprung into action so quickly that it shocked me. Like she'd been struck by a bolt of inspiration lightning. Everyone stopped moving or hushed the conversations that were still happening in the background and those who could see her stared at Melinda.

She turned to me and said, "Tawny, I'm so sorry but I'm going to have to cut our visit short if I'm going to pull this off by the time that Dario gets here. He's going to love seeing the house all decorated." Then she walked off towards the entrance, leaving me behind. But her path was stopped by Muffy, who came bounding in the room and knocked Melinda over.

"That dog!" she exclaimed. "I don't know how Auntie Elise handled being around her."

Muffy was closely followed by Leonardo who was running so fast after the dog that he skidded on the floor trying to come to a stop and chase her through the lounge.

But it was too late. Muffy found me on the couch and jumped on me. She was licking my face like it had peanut butter on it.

"Muffy!" Melinda yelled, picking herself up off the ground. "Leonardo! Get that dog under control!"

"Yes ma'am," he said, now trying to wrangle Muffy off of me.

I laughed and pet Muffy, which seemed to calm her down. "It's okay!" I said, trying to assure everyone that I was fine. I loved dogs so it really wasn't an issue. Muffy was just a little playful is all.

As Leonardo grabbed her by the collar, dragging her off the couch, Muffy's paw bumped my phone from where it was sitting facedown. I gasped, completely forgetting the dog and chasing the phone that was now skittering across the floor face-up. The screen was locked but it still showed that it was recording on the lock screen.

It was heading right for Melinda.

But me chasing the phone made Muffy think that we were playing a game. She broke free from Leonardo's grip and tried to catch me. Muffy reached the phone first. Thankfully it was before it had a chance to get to Melinda.

I was nervous she was going to pick it up with her mouth like it was a ball and chomp down on it, but she didn't. Instead, Muffy stopped suddenly, her body going completely rigid, and pointed her nose in the direction of the phone. Thankfully, Muffy's body blocked the phone from Melinda, making it easy for me to grab.

"Thanks, girl." I said, patting Muffy on the head. She relaxed her stance and licked my hand. Leonardo walked up to her again, grabbing her collar and dragging her out of the room while Melinda said, "Tawny! I'm so sorry. Is your phone okay? I'll buy you a new one if she broke it."

"It's fine," I said, inspecting my phone and was truly shocked that it was in fact fine. I pressed stop on the recording from the lock screen in case it somehow escaped my possession again.

"Good! I don't know what I'm going to do with that dog," Melinda sighed. "Or any of Auntie Elise's pets for the matter. The rest are relatively well-behaved but that one, she's got too much energy."

It made me sad to see Muffy getting dragged away when all she wanted to do was play. "I'm sure she'll mellow out. There's just been a lot of activity the last few days, ya know?" I tried to reassure Melinda. "How did she know to point at the phone like that?" I asked, curiosity getting the better of me.

"She's a hunting dog of some kind. Leonardo, what's the breed again?" she asked.

"A German Shorthaired Pointer, ma'am," he said through gritted teeth, trying to manage Muffy.

"More like a shorthaired monster if you ask me," Melinda laughed. "Okay well, sorry to be a terrible hostess and rush you out like this, but you understand. You can see yourself out?" She asked as she walked away, but she didn't wait for an answer before disappearing around a corner.

Chapter 22

As soon as Melinda was gone, I unlocked my phone to double check that the recording had been saved. Then I uploaded it to the cloud so that there was no chance of deleting it. But I'd forgotten about the terrible reception up here. It would take forever to upload. I had to get down the hill.

It was pretty clear that Melinda was throwing this party to impress Dario, not out of grief or out of some rush to try and hurry the settling of her aunt's affairs. So it didn't strike me as the behavior of a guilty woman, just a lovesick one; someone who was trying to impress her boyfriend.

I walked out to my car, and the activity in the house was just as busy as before but this time there was a frantic energy. Before getting in my car, I did one more look around to see if Muffy was hanging out anywhere. I was a little sad when I realized that she was nowhere to be seen.

Maybe it was time to start thinking about getting a dog. I'd always wanted one, but in Los Angeles I wasn't home often enough to get one. Now, I was almost always at the studio. If I was gone, it wasn't for long, only a few hours here and there. And it would be nice to have a running companion, too.

On the walk to my car, I couldn't help but laugh at how the mood of everything had changed. There were people quickly unloading the trucks they'd almost nearly finished loading minutes ago. Leonardo Casa was directing people like a conductor. It was as if they were all in a race to set up a party faster than ever before.

As soon as I started up my car, I got a text from Jessica. Not wanting to text on the winding road while driving, I stopped and read it.

JESSICA: I'm coming home tomorrow. Want to work-out in the morning then catch me up?

TAWNY: Yup! And clear your schedule because Melinda is holding a memorial party at the house.

JESSICA: Intriguing! Can't wait to hear all about it.

Since she kept the conversation short, I figured she was texting in between scenes and decided to save the details until tomorrow. Besides, it would look weird if I was idling in the driveway much longer.

On my way back into town, I called Sheriff Jackson. I'd already spent enough time at the station for one day and didn't feel like being there any longer than I had to, so a phone call would have to suffice. There was something about police stations that always made me feel instantly depressed. If a gray cloud was a building, it would be a police station.

Sheriff Jackson picked up on the first ring. "Shantytown Sheriff's Station. Sheriff Jackson speaking. How can I help you?"

"Wow, this is *the* Sheriff Jackson? Don't you have someone there who can answer the phones for you?" I teased.

"They're at lunch," he answered and though he sounded unamused, I could sense a smile in his tone. "So what did you find out, Monroe?"

Back to business. "Not too much. Dario wasn't in town when Elise died. He was apparently on the way *into* town but was stuck in a storm that delayed his flight from New York," I explained. "You should have your people follow up on that when they get back."

"Will do," he said. "Anything else interesting?"

"She wasn't giving me much so I asked whether there would be a funeral or memorial. Since she stands to inherit so much, I figured a rush to settle everything would make her seem more suspicious," I explained.

"Smart thinking. And?" he sounded eager.

"Well, she jumped at the idea of a memorial and is fine with the funeral taking as long as it needs to. It seems like

Melinda's biggest concern is impressing Dario; for the time being, anyway," I sighed, suddenly feeling overwhelmingly tired after a bad night of sleep. "Oh, and one more thing. She said she was staying at a hotel in town leading up to the tea party and only arrived a little before the start time listed on the invites. She said she was in the maze because no one could find her aunt and they used to often walk in there together."

"Interesting. What's your gut say?"

"Despite all of the circumstantial evidence, she just doesn't seem capable of doing something like this," I sighed. "I'd say we keep our options open, but I just don't think she did it.

"We'll confirm which hotel she was staying in and when she left," he noted. "So when's the memorial?"

"Tomorrow." I was curious about what his reaction would be, since it had struck me as hasty. But then again, she'd only thought of it after I prompted her.

"Okay then," he replied in his calm, measured tone.

"Does anything ever surprise you?" I asked.

"If you don't expect anything then nothing is a surprise. I just go along with what is right in front of me."

"Wow. I wasn't expecting something that profound," I said genuinely shocked.

"See? That's because you had a mental expectation. Learn to go with the flow, Monroe."

"Was that a joke?" I asked.

"I don't know. Were you expecting one?" He returned. I wasn't sure what was happening here. Were we both really being this corny while flirting? Did this even count as flirting? It was more like an awkward conversation. I must have taken a second too long to respond because he said, "I'll see you at the memorial tomorrow then?"

"Yup, I'll be there," I answered.

"I'll talk to you then unless something else comes up first. Bye, Monroe," he said and hung up before I had a chance to respond. I wasn't sure if that was a good thing or not, but decided not to give it too much thought. Why put expectations on something unnecessarily?

Chapter 23

I pulled into the parking lot in front of my fitness studio and walked inside instead of going up to the apartment.

My afternoons were usually packed with client after client, so having free time felt unfamiliar. Not quite sure what to do with myself, I took the opportunity to tackle a "to do" that I always dreaded: bookkeeping. It wasn't that it was hard — in fact it was pretty straightforward for a personal trainer, much more than it had been as a private investigator — it was just monotonous and time consuming. But now was the perfect opportunity to do it.

So I turned on some music, sat down at my desk, and got to work. First I looked at my schedule and matched payments to each client. These last few weeks had been busy because everyone wanted to look their best for the tea party.

That's when I realized it had been about a week since Lady Sinclair was in here for a session, which was odd. She was usually booked five days a week if not more. Had she been training with my business rival Duncan Harris? After finding out her secret about Scott, I wasn't sure what to believe. But I quickly talked myself down from that train of thought. Lady Sinclair had been the first of Duncan's clients to defect and come to my studio. Since then, she'd brought lots more clientele my way. There's no way she'd go back to train with him.

It was still odd that she hadn't been in though, nor scheduled her next appointment. I pulled out my phone and dialed Lady Sinclair's number. She picked up on the first ring and launched into conversation. "Tawny, you'll have to excuse all of the background noise," she said at a tone just below a yell. "I'm over at Elise's house helping Melinda set up for the memorial. Oh, actually, I guess it's no longer Elise's house, is it? Anyways, I'm here now. She mentioned it was your idea. To have the memorial."

"I don't think I can take credit for that. I was only curious about *if* there was going to be some kind of service," I tried to play it off. "I mentioned it would be a waste to have to bring back all of the tables and chairs since they were already there."

"Great point. So to what do I owe this call?" Lady Sinclar asked, sounding distracted.

"Well I was just going over my schedule and I realized you hadn't been into the studio for a week. I know how disciplined you are about your fitness regimen. Do you want to put something on the calendar?"

"My God, I think you're right!" Lady Sinclair gasped. "Yes, please! With everything going on, our sessions completely slipped my mind. How about the day after the memorial?"

"Sounds good. I'll put you down for the usual 9am slot." I was secretly glad that we'd be meeting *after* the memorial and that Lady Sinclair hadn't tried to squeeze in a session beforehand. That way I could hear any new murder-related gossip that Lady Sinclair gathered at the memorial.

"Tawny, I've got to go. See you tomorrow," Lady Sinclair said abruptly. In the background I could hear some kind of commotion and she hung up.

After penciling in Lady Sinclair's appointment, I looked ahead to tomorrow morning and my session with Jessica. I took a few more minutes to write out the workout I had planned for her to do, then locked up the studio, and walked upstairs to my apartment.

I flopped down on the couch, all of a sudden feeling exhausted. I must have been more tired than I realized because the next thing I knew, my alarm was going off.

Chapter 24

I looked at the clock. It was 6 a.m. And despite somehow sleeping for 12 hours straight, I hit the snooze button. But I never really fell back asleep. So I got up, put on my shoes, and went for a run. Since I'd fallen asleep much earlier than I meant to, I felt discombobulated. Luckily running always helped clear my mind and get me ready for the day. I mentally started making a plan of attack to get everything done.

Before I knew it, I'd finished running my loop and was back home. I showered, got dressed, and hopped in my car en route to Jessica's house.

Jessica lived up in the hills like Elise did, but it was the hills on the other side of town. The scenery on the drive was similar though. Winding streets that were easy to get lost in if you didn't know where you were going. I'd been here enough times that I finally had the route memorized.

But no matter how often I came here, I was always impressed when I pulled in through the gate and up the long, tree-lined driveway.

It took a long time before I felt comfortable using the code to open the gate instead of pressing the button to be buzzed in. It felt like walking in someone's front door or something. But Jessica begged me to use the code so she didn't have to find the remote every time I came over.

Jessica's house looked like the big mansions in Pasadena that you'd see in movies like "The Graduate." Except hers wasn't on a residential street; it was hidden in the coastal wilderness.

I parked in front of the house and knocked on the door. It was an impressively huge door to match the imposing house. The door was so thick that it barely made a sound when I knocked. Much like the gate, Jessica always told me to walk right inside. But this literally was just walking into someone's home, so I never felt comfortable doing it without at least knocking.

Sure enough, after I knocked, the intercom at the door crackled to life with Jessica's voice saying, "Come on in. We're in the kitchen!" Despite how stunning the house was, it was an older build, and the intercom system couldn't be updated without tearing out the walls. The same was true of the intercom down at the gate, which was why she was still using a remote to let people in.

I followed instructions and walked inside to the kitchen — a giant, industrial-looking space with huge appliances. This house was unique in that it had a traditional exterior but the interior had been totally re-done with modern decor. I saw Jessica standing there in matching black leggings and a sports bra. She was dwarfed by the large size of her surroundings.

Since she was my best friend, I saw her often, but I was often struck by how beautiful she was. Sometimes actors look completely different off-screen than they do on-screen, but not Jessica. She was somehow even more alluring in person. I always thought the warm energy she exuded added to her good looks too. Anyone who was around her instantly felt better, like a little sliver of sunshine shone into their life.

In the kitchen, Jessica was chatting with her live-in boyfriend Lloyd Charles. As gorgeous as Jessica was, Lloyd was somehow equally handsome. He was in his mid-30s and still had the body of a collegiate athlete, with short blonde hair, a golden tan, and a smile that could blind someone. To top it off, he was also super nice and fun to be around, which meant that as much as people may have wanted to hate this stunning A-list couple, it was impossible to because they were so kind. They were friendly to everyone, and not just because they didn't want bad press.

Since Lloyd was also an actor, he traveled a lot for work, too. That's why when they were both in Shantytown, they made it a priority to spend time together. But one of the places where Jessica drew the line of togetherness was couples workouts. She took this time very seriously, saying it was the one opportunity she had to check in with her body and relax her mind. If Lloyd was working out with her, there would be a social aspect introduced which Jessica didn't want.

That's why it was no surprise when Jessica told me we needed to talk about everything that had happened with the murder, but not until after the workout. She wanted to stay focused and centered and work off some of the energy from a week of shooting. Jessica planted a kiss on Lloyd's cheek and walked towards the french doors leading to the backyard.

Lloyd jokingly yelled after us, "Okay then! I'll see you later, hon. Bye, Tawny!"

"See ya, Lloyd," I shouted back, already halfway out of the door.

Weather permitting — and it usually was in Shantytown — Jessica preferred to have our sessions outside in full sunlight. It was a gorgeous day, so she unrolled her yoga mat on a patch of grass next to the pool.

I took the paper out of my pocket where I'd written the routine for the day — pilates, Jessica's favorite. It was a full 60-minute sweat fest, with lots of heart rate-raising core work, and by the end Jessica was spent. I had to admit, I was tired just from walking her through all of that.

Afterward Jessica laid on her mat, exhausted, and said, "Okay, *now* you have to tell me everything about what we've got going on today. How did this even happen?"

Chapter 25

There was a lot of story to tell since she'd been out of town, but I skipped to the relevant highlights. I told her the story of how I'd gone to Melinda's to sneakily record her. Then how I accidentally ended up giving her the idea to have a memorial, and Melinda had jumped at the chance so she could show it off to her boyfriend.

"Wow, that's a lot," Jessica said, sitting up now that she'd had enough time to cool down. "So the memorial is what we have to get ready for today?"

I nodded.

"Do you think the boyfriend will be there? What was his name again? Dario? Kind of a cool name, right?" Jessica mused.

"I hadn't thought of it, but yeah I guess it is a pretty cool name. And yeah, the hope is that he'll be there, both for Melinda's sake and for the investigation," I said.

"And tell me if I've got this straight. The whole point of you and I going to the memorial is to see if we can tell if

Dario had anything to do with this *and* to scope out the crowd to see if the killer shows up?" Jessica asked, then took a sip of her water.

"Yup, that sums it up," I answered. "But mostly the latter. At this point, figuring out if Dario is involved is up to the sheriff now. Scott is also one of our suspects. Oh, and when I found Elise, she had some substance in her mouth. It turned out to be chlorine," I explained.

"She was *poisoned*?" Jessica gasped, clapping a hand over her mouth.

I shook my head. "That's what I thought too but there was no sign of chlorine in her body. Only on her mouth."

She paused to think. "Well that's super weird." I nodded in agreement.

Then Jessica got up abruptly and started rolling up her yoga mat. "Okay well I'm going to go upstairs and shower. And it looks like," she pointed her finger at me waving it the length of my body, "Judging by the lack of a bag in your hand, I'm guessing you could use an outfit to wear to the memorial."

I looked at her in mock offense, but I knew she was right. I'd put in the barest of minimal efforts before coming over here, completely forgetting I'd have to go to the memorial straight from here. "You know me well," I said.

"Come up to my room with me and pick something out," Jessica said, leading us back into the house. Lloyd was nowhere to be seen but it was a big house so that wasn't unusual.

Jessica's closet was as big as my entire apartment, complete with a little sitting area inside of it. I looked at all of the gorgeous designer dresses hanging in it, and couldn't decide which to wear. It was a memorial after all so of course we'd be wearing black. I had apparently taken longer than I thought because by the time Jessica was out of the shower, I was still in there browsing.

"You never were very good at being decisive," Jessica laughed. "I had a feeling you'd still be looking, but I have a perfect one in mind for you." She swept through a few different options, eventually landing on a long-sleeved black shift dress. It wasn't tight but it wasn't unflattering either; it really was perfect. "And you can wear these," Jessica walked over to the floor-to-ceiling shoe rack and tossed me a pair of black pumps. With friends like her, who needed to shop? Especially when I'd lucked out and we were the same size in everything.

"This is great, Jess. Thanks!" I felt excited to put the new-to-me clothes on. Jessica picked something similar but with a different hem and neckline so that we didn't match.

A few minutes later, we were ready to leave. But there had still been no sign of Lloyd. Jessica walked to the intercom box on the wall and said, "Lloyd." Then released the button and gave it a few seconds before trying again. "Lloyd!" saying it louder this time.

His voice came through, with lots of background noise. "Hey Jess! I'm upstairs playing video games."

"Okay well we're leaving. I'll be back in a few hours. Love you!" she said and started walking away, not waiting for a response.

But one did come through, saying, "Sounds good. Love you, too!" Then he was back to his game.

Chapter 26

We hopped into Jessica's silver G-Wagen and tapped in the address to the Huntington-Wilbury estate. Once that was in the GPS, we were on our way

I assumed the memorial had a larger guest list than the party since this was less exclusive than the annual soirée, but the line of cars was much more tame than the first time I'd been up here. That made me a little sad. Sure, the memorial was short notice so maybe some people genuinely couldn't make it. But it was a bummer to think that some people were more interested in going to a party than saying goodbye to someone who considered them to be friends. Then again, we were still a bit early.

As we pulled up, Louis the valet was diligently standing by and opened my passenger door before running around to Jessica's side. Then I noticed Sheriff Jackson's car off to the side near where the vans were loading up the other day.

It was hard to make a sheriff's car incognito but he'd tried to as well as he could. I looked around to see where he was. No sight of him in the front yard. He must have been inside the house.

As soon as Louis was out of earshot of us, Jessica leaned in and asked, "So what is it I should be looking for today?"

I thought about it before answering. "I'm not sure it'll be any one thing. Just keep an eye out for people who look out of place or suspicious."

Jessica nodded, indicating that she understood the assignment. She also did some sort of mock military gesture, using two fingers to point at her eyes, then flipped them and pointed straight ahead. It made me laugh out loud.

There was a man standing at the door with a tray of full tea cups in his hand. We walked towards him and each took a cup, nodding in thanks.

"This was a nice tribute," I raised the cup.

"Makes me wonder if it means Melinda is doing *too* much to seem sympathetic, like a *guilty* person would," Jessica suggested, narrowing her eyes.

I laughed, "Take it easy there, Columbo. We have to keep an open mind. It's easy to think everyone looks guilty, but hard to undo that once you've thought it." I'd learned that lesson more than once chasing down dead end leads because I'd convinced myself someone was the culprit when they weren't at all.

"I always forget how grand this place is," Jessica said, as we walked in.

I agreed, once again stunned by the majesty. "Yeah, that's a great word for it. Grand."

"It's a shame Elise only had people up here once a year," Jessica mused.

Once we were past the door, we were greeted by the mild chaos of people who were setting the event. I wasn't sure where to look or what to do, so I was relieved when Lady Sinclair's voice called out, saving us from awkwardly standing around.

"Tawny! Is that you?" She trilled from another room.

I couldn't see where her voice was coming from so I just shouted, "Yeah! I'm here with Jessica. We thought we'd come early and help set up," — and snoop around, I thought to myself.

Lady Sinclair rounded the corner from the kitchen and appeared in front of us. "Jessica! You're here too. This is a surprise," she walked over giving Jessica the traditional European two-cheek kiss hello then bestowed the same greeting to me. "Aren't you both dolls for wanting to help. Everything is almost done but if you want something to do, I suppose you can arrange the guestbook table."

"Sure! We can do that. Where is it?" I asked, looking around, but didn't see a table anywhere.

Lady Sinclair waved us towards the yard. "Out in the back. That's actually where the memorial will be held. Melinda was setting it up inside, but I put an end to that as soon as I arrived. Poor thing didn't think twice about all those people traipsing through Elise's house," she explained. "I don't know what I expected from an *influencer* though. Can you believe that's a real job? In any case, you'll find the table out there," she pointed to the yard where a giant canopy had been erected with rows of chairs underneath.

There wasn't any rain predicted in the weather, but if a marine layer rolled in off the ocean, it could get misty very quickly. On the other hand, if the sun decided to shine in its full glory, it would bake the attendees. So a canopy was a perfect idea.

From the amount of chairs I saw set up, it looked like they were expecting quite a few people. I wondered how many would overlap with the guestlist from the tea party.

As we passed through the kitchen to get to the back door, Jessica nudged me and whispered, "Who's the sheriff talking to over there?" nodding towards the breakfast nook in the kitchen.

I looked over and sure enough there was Sheriff Jackson talking to a man who looked very much like Dario Schmid's Instagram profile picture. "I think that's Dario

Schimd, Melinda's boyfriend. I guess his plane finally made it here."

"And just in time for his girlfriend to inherit a huge chunk of cash," Jessica noted.

The two men seem to be in a serious conversation, but not a contentious one. There was no chance of us over-hearing them, and I knew Sheriff Jackson would fill me in later. So we quietly crept outside, careful not to disturb them.

Then suddenly out of nowhere something hit me hard in the chest and knocked me to the ground.

Chapter 27

"Tawny!" Jessica yelled and tried to catch me.

I scrambled to get my bearings and to figure out if I was hurt and what had hit me. Other than my butt aching from the fall I was fine, but I couldn't get up. I was being held down! Then it became clear why: Muffy had planted herself right on my chest and was licking my face.

"Muffy!" I laughed and patted her head, trying to push her to the side so I could get up.

As usual Leonardo was five steps behind the big dog and arrived too late. "Muffy! Get over here!" he demanded but the dog didn't even seem to notice him. "I am so sorry, Ms. Monroe. She must remember you from the other day."

"It's fine" I smiled but looked at Muffy and in a stern voice said, "No jumping." Her ears lost a bit of their perk and she seemed to understand she'd done something wrong.

Leonardo grabbed her by the collar again and dragged her down the hall. "You're going in the garage for the rest of the day," he chided.

"Are you okay?" Jessica asked.

"Yeah, just a little sore but I'll live." I caught Sheriff Jackson's eye from across the kitchen. Then he quickly drew his gaze away from me and back to his conversation with Dario.

There had been so much commotion overall that the incident had barely interrupted the two men aside from drawing minimal attention to us.

The guestbook table was off to the side of the yard near where the entrance for the tea party had been. The only thing that indicated this was the guestbook table was a large white notebook set on top of it. No signs, pens, or anything were provided for people.

So we set about borrowing decorations from other places in the yard — we took some flowers from the arrangements up front, we swiped some tablecloths from some tables along the edges where people likely wouldn't go anyway, and a letterboard sign from the decorator's truck parked in the driveway. It only took about 20 minutes until both of us were happy with how the table looked.

"Do we just stand here now? There's nowhere to sit." Jessica noted. "I have to admit, I'm a little worn out from that workout this morning."

I hadn't even thought about the lack of chairs. "No one will miss a couple of those," I said pointing to the rows of chairs that were all set up looking towards a makeshift stage. I took two for the back row nearest us and put them behind the table.

"We'll get a good look at people from here when they come in. But we should just stay in the back even when the service starts so we can see how everyone is acting, too," Jessica proposed.

"Great idea. Though, I think the killer might try to sneak in if they're trying to go unnoticed," I said.

"At the very least we'll get to see everyone's outfit," Jessica laughed.

We kept scanning the setup to see if there was anything interesting or suspicious happening, but after a few minutes of chatting, we got lost in catching up. We kept going over the theories, top suspects, and evidence that was gathered so far. Jessica was great at piecing things together so I wanted her to have the same information I did in case I had any blind spots. But she picked up on something I hadn't planned.

"So you've been spending a lot of time with Sheriff Jackson then?" she asked, her eyebrows raised.

I could feel myself blushing. "What do you mean? I'm helping out with the case, so it makes sense we'd be working together on this."

Jessica crossed her arms. "Tawny, you've mentioned him in about every other sentence you've said. 'Sheriff Jackson' this, 'Sheriff Jackson' that. Admit it. You have a crush on this guy," she playfully slapped me on the knee.

"I do not!" I protested, but even I knew it came out with a little too much force. "I mean, yeah, he's handsome. But lots of men are handsome." Then I spotted Scott across the lawn. "Look over there!" I whispered to Jessica, even though there was no one around to hear us.

"That guy? Yeah I guess he's handsome. But you can't just point at any guy. I know what you're trying to do," Jessica clearly didn't get the point.

"No!" I laughed. "I'm not saying — nevermind. Look, there's Scott Summers! The poolboy!" I pointed towards the side road that led down to the staff parking lot.

"Ooooh. Lady Sinclair's booty call," Jessica joked.

"I think she would have a heart attack if she heard you call him that," I laughed imagining her reaction..

"Okay, but seriously, so he's the main suspect right now?" she asked.

I shook my head. "Not really. Kind of. Besides Dario, who Sheriff Jackson is talking to in the in the kitchen."

"There you go again talking about Sheriff Jackson," Jessica winked. "Anyways, see anyone milling around here who you'd suspected?"

I looked around but only saw the usual staff members. The gardener was trimming the already pristine hedges, the house manager was directing some of the other staff I'd seen floating around the other times I was here, the same caterers that had been here during the tea party were here now. Nothing seemed out of the ordinary.

Then Jessica spotted someone in what looked like a baggy white hazmat suit. It was fully covering their body, including their head. The figure was walking up a grassy hill, holding a box of some kind in their hand.

"Is that... a beekeeper?" I asked.

"Oh yes, *her*," Lady Sinclair's voice came from behind me, making me jump. She didn't seem to notice my reaction though and said, "Elise only liked fresh, raw honey with her tea. So she has her own bee colony on-site. It also helps with all the looming colony collapses or whatever." Lady Sinclair waved it off as though it was nonsense.

"Lady Sinclair! You snuck up on us," I laughed.

"I'm everywhere, darling," she smiled. "Anyways, the guestbook table looks great," she said, giving it a once over.

"Thanks! We figured we'd sit back here to make sure everyone signed in," Jessica explained. "You know how it is when you get somewhere and easily miss something like the guest book."

"Yes. Yes, of course. That sounds like a great idea. Well, I'm off to go... Oh, you know," Lady Sinclair said a little coldly and waved her hand, gesturing at nothing in particular. Then she floated off again towards the front of the house.

There wasn't bad blood between Jessica and Lady Sinclair, but I'd noticed that it always seemed like it was hard for Lady Sinclair to let her guard down around the younger actress. It was like Jessica reminded her too much of her glory days.

It wasn't even five minutes later that people started trickling in and Jessica and I were ushering them towards the guestbook. At first, the people arriving were mostly people I didn't recognize, which wasn't too surprising since I was still new in town. Then after a while, some of Shantytown's more famous faces showed up. Once this more well-known group arrived, Lady Sinclair joined Jessica and I to welcome them.

I kept scanning the crowd for anyone who looked out of the ordinary or was acting odd. Then I realized someone very conspicuous was missing from the crowd: Sheriff

Jackson. I didn't dare mention it to Jessica, lest she start testing me again. But I realized I never saw him leave the house after questioning Dario. From what I could gather, both of them were still inside. Now that I thought about it, I hadn't even caught a glimpse of Melinda all day.

For a brief second I wondered if Sheriff Jackson had decided to take the couple down to the station for more questioning. But if that was the case, I'd think he would have texted me since that would be disruptive to the service if the niece and heir to the estate wouldn't be attending her aunt's memorial. And besides, Lady Sinclair would have known if that happened and told us immediately since she loved a scandal.

Finally the seats were half full and the harpist near the podium at the front started playing. The local priest, Father Timothy Monk, got up from his seat off to the side and walked up to the front to start the memorial ceremony.

Even after the line slowed and we didn't have to guide as many people to the guest book, we didn't leave our post. It gave us a great view of the entire scene. Somehow though, we'd missed Melinda and Dario slipping into their seats at the front. Maybe Melinda just didn't feel like talking to a bunch of people that were her aunt's friends, not hers, especially while she was grieving. There was still no sign of Sheriff Jackson though.

Just then I spotted an unfamiliar mousy woman with shoulder-length brown hair sitting towards the back on the side where the audience was more sparse. She didn't look like she fit with this crowd. Being a glitterati outsider myself, it was easy to tell.

The woman looked around, then quietly got up and walked towards the house.

Her head was on a swivel as if to make sure no one was watching her. I nudged Jessica to make sure she was seeing this. She nodded and sprang into action.

Chapter 28

After the woman disappeared into the house, Jessica ran towards the back door in pursuit. She crept around some tall shrubs, and carefully followed the woman inside. I decided it was okay to leave my post for a minute and follow. It turned out the backdoor was a perfect vantage point, because I could see inside but also keep an eye on what was going on outside in case another suspicious figure presented themself.

Everyone seemed to be attentively watching Father Monk, who was speaking at the front of the crowd, but I noticed there were very few tears. Turning my attention back to the house, I peered inside but there was no sign of Jessica nor the woman.

At that moment, I spotted Sheriff Jackson appearing from the foyer, inching towards the stairs. He looked towards the back doorway and saw me. He smiled, put his finger to his lips indicating to be quiet, then disappeared up the stairs. I wondered if it was just in my head, or if his smile had been a little warmer than usual, like he was happy to see me standing there. I shook the thought from my head. I had to stay focused on finding this woman and Jessica, not daydreaming about a cute man.

I assumed that Jessica and the woman had gone upstairs and the sheriff was following them. But I was hesitant to leave my spot — what if that woman was some kind of decoy and the real killer was still out there in the crowd? If I moved, we'd lose our chance to spot them. But that would mean this was some kind of conspiracy and we had no evidence to suggest that was true.

Then suddenly there was a crashing sound from upstairs. It was so loud that Father Monk stopped talking, momentarily distracted by the commotion. People in the audience turned their heads to see what was going on.

Unfortunately, all they were able to see was me awkwardly standing in the doorway. Unsure of what to do, I waved and shrugged while mentally trying to make myself so small that I hoped I would disappear. After realizing I wasn't a magician and was still in the same spot, I motioned to everyone that I was going inside to see what happened. They seemed uninterested and slowly all turned around towards the front again. Father Monk took the hint and resumed talking. I spotted Melinda staring at me, but I couldn't make out her expression behind her oversized sunglasses.

I darted inside and ran up the stairs, no longer concerned about making too much noise. I gasped when I saw the scene at the top of the staircase.

Chapter 29

I had to cover my mouth to keep from laughing at what I saw. Jessica and the woman were rolling around on the ground, wrestling over an object that was obscured by both of their hands.

Sheriff Jackson was standing over them, verbally trying to get them to separate with some firm, "Ladies... LADIES..." commands. They either didn't hear him or didn't care because they kept right at it. I tried to get a peek at what they were fighting over but it was impossible to tell with all of the movement and arms flailing.

Jessica finally caught a glimpse of me and said, "We've got her!" As she said it, she triumphantly held up a reusable nylon grocery shopping bag for everyone to see.

"And what is that, Ms. Harrington?" Sheriff Jackson asked. It looked like he was trying to hold back a laugh. I had to admit, the sight of Hollywood's leading lady holding up a clumsy nylon sack after wresting it from a local woman was pretty comical. To make it even more amusing, Jessica had no clue what was in her hand.

She looked at the sack, clearly just taking it in for the first time. "Well, it's uh... a bag! *Obviously*. And there's this inside it!" Jessica reached into the bag and pulled out a silver candlestick. She looked at it for a second, confusion crossing her face, but then she quickly recovered her look of triumph. "She's the one who did it! And she's here to steal back the evidence"

Meanwhile the woman remained lying on the ground looking worse for the wear, and a bit scared.

"Are you insinuating this woman killed Mrs. Huntington-Wilbury with a candlestick in the garden?" Sheriff Jackson asked, striving to use his serious tone.

"Insinuating I *what*?" the woman jumped up, suddenly coming to life. "Look, I don't know what all this is about, but I didn't kill anyone." She started walking towards the stairs like she was going to try and make a getaway, but I stood in the way, cutting her off.

"Oh yeah? Then why are you at the funeral acting all sneaky and stealing evidence?" Jessica pointedly asked, once again holding the candlestick aloft in triumph before shoving it back in the bag.

"How about I take it from here?" Sheriff Jackson said, reaching to take the bag from Jessica who readily handed it over. He looked at the woman, "What is your name?" he asked her.

"I don't see how that's relevant," she said, smoothing out her plain black dress and looking over her shoulder as though looking for another way out of here.

"You have been caught stealing from the home of a woman who was likely murdered. However overzealous Ms. Harrington may have been in her pursuit, she's right that you're potentially stealing evidence," he shot a look at Jessica. She was not happy about being labeled "overzealous" and made it clear by crossing her arms in protest. "So you can tell me your name now, or I can take you down to the station and question you there."

The woman waved her hands as though to ward off even the insinuation of being taken to the Sheriff's Station. "There's no need for all of that." She looked deflated. "My name is Jane Goodall."

"You've got to be kidding me," Jessica blurted, and Sheriff Jackson shot her another look to be quiet.

"I know, I know. It sounds like a fake name, but I swear that's my name. My mother was an animal lover. Look, I can show you my ID if you don't believe me," she said and reached into the pocket of her dress. A look of panic crossed Jane's face, indicating that the wallet wasn't there. She turned around, trying to find it and spotted it on the floor of the hallway. She bent over to get it. "Sorry, it must have fallen out when I was *attacked*," she sneered at Jessica, who started to respond, but stopped when Sheriff Jackson shook his head at her as though saying, "Don't." Then he reached for the wallet and looked at the ID.

I could see "Jane" written on the ID from over the sheriff's shoulder but not the last name. "Okay, Ms. Goodall, can you explain what's going on here?" he handed her back her ID, satisfied that her name was correct.

Jane Goodall sighed. "Well, money's been a little tight at home. With prices going up, it's not easy living in this town if you aren't rich and famous," shooting Jessica an accusatory look. "I was at DINE and heard that this memorial was happening. I figured I'd come and see if there was an opportunity to get inside and take a couple of things I could pawn. Nothing too valuable like art or jewelry, just something like this silver candlestick. But I didn't plan on getting *jumped*," she added, trying to reinforce that she was the victim here.

"So you didn't know Ms. Huntington-Wilbury? And you weren't at her tea party when she died?" Sheriff Jackson asked.

"No! I'd only heard all of the same stories about her as everyone else had, about how she was an eccentric. So I figured she'd have some unique and valuable things," Jane explained.

"I believe you, Ms. Goodall, but you've also broken the law," he said.

Jane started to cry. "Please don't send me to jail. I'm so sorry. I know I shouldn't have done it. I just don't have any other options. I'm already working two jobs to put food on the table. I've got three kids and my husband left years ago. So there's not even enough money to move somewhere else. Please Sheriff..." she trailed off. My heart broke for this woman, and I made a mental note to see if there was a way I could help her out.

"Like I was saying, you broke the law. *But* you were stopped before any significant damage could be done. So I'll let you off this time," he finished.

"Thank you, Sheriff. I promise this is the last time you'll see me," Jane said, bringing her hands to her chest in gratitude.

"I hope that's true. Unless of course we're both in town, in which case please say hello. We're still neighbors," he tipped his hat to her, then moved out of the way, motioning to the stairs. "You can go. But you need to leave the premises immediately. Don't go back to the service," he instructed.

Jane thanked him again and shuffled down the stairs.

Jessica's fury had subsided and she looked as culled as I felt. There was something truly heartbreaking about someone so desperate that they'd risk everything. "You know, sometimes I'm in my own little world so much that I forget there are problems right here in our little town," Jessica noted.

"There are lots of places you can volunteer if you're interested," Sheriff Jackson offered. "I'll tell you about them later. But right now, we should all get back to observing the memorial. Seeing if any other leads pop up. Oh, and Ms. Harrington," he handed Jessica the bag with the candlestick, "Would you put this back where it came from?"

Jessica nodded yes and took it, disappearing into the nearest doorway and emerging with only the bag. "What do I do with this?"

"Souvenir," he said. "From your first citizen's arrest."

Chapter 30

We headed back to the memorial, keeping a watchful eye on the crowd, but unfortunately it didn't reveal any new leads. Everything proceeded as planned, and I thought that overall it was a really nice sendoff for Elise. Afterward Jessica and I found Sheriff Jackson standing off to the side of the exit, taking mental stock of who was leaving. "Well, as far as identifying suspects, that was a bust. So what's next?" I asked.

Sheriff Jackson scratched his head and said, "We're running short on leads here. Dario's flights all checked out, but I haven't asked him about the Ponzi scheme yet. Didn't want to play all of my cards at once and potentially ruin the service."

"That's smart," I acknowledged.

"You sound surprised," he mused.

If I was being honest, I was surprised a small town sheriff would be thinking that strategically, but I didn't want to let him know that. I knew it was my "big-city bias" creeping in. "Not at all. Just... impressed, I guess," I finally said.

Melinda was standing near the back but not quite at the exit, shaking hands and chatting with people as they were leaving. The mood was less somber than I was used to seeing at memorials. People seemed to be really talkative and there were still very few tears. But then again that shouldn't have been too surprising from what I could tell, since not many people were close to Ms. Huntington-Wilbury.

Dario was standing near Melinda but away from the people, tapping away on his phone. Sheriff Jackson walked over to him. Jessica and I exchanged a conspiratory glance, then followed. We pretended to be cleaning up but in reality we just wanted to get close enough to hear their conversation. We had to strain but could pick up the gist of it.

Sheriff Jackson let Dario know that he was going to have to come back to the station to answer some more questions. Melinda's voice could be heard clear as a bell. "Is that entirely necessary? He answered all of your questions earlier." She sounded exasperated.

"I still have a few more for him," Sheriff Jackson calmly said, careful not to give anything away.

"Am I under arrest?" Dario asked. He sounded every bit as entitled as I'd imagined he would.

"No, not right now. But if you don't voluntarily come with me, I have no problem putting you under arrest to get you to the station," Sheriff Jackson answered, and once again I found myself in awe of how even-keeled the Sheriff was under any circumstance.

"Arrest for what?!" Melinda demanded.

Sheriff Jackson waited a beat, giving Dario one last chance to agree to go on his own, but he didn't budge. "On charges to defraud Elise Huntington-Wilbury."

The color drained from Dario's face and he gulped so hard that I could see it even from where I was standing.

"Defraud Aunt Elise? What is he talking about, Dario?" Melinda asked, less offended and more confused than she sounded before.

"This is ridiculous. I have no idea what he's talking about," Dario pulled himself back together, acting over-ly-confident. But he complied anyway. "I'll go with you Sheriff, if only to put all of this behind us. You're upsetting Melinda, and she's been through enough."

"I'm glad we see eye to eye," Sheriff Jackson said and led Dario to the car.

Melinda walked over to me and Jessica. "Do you know what in the world that's about?" She looked like she was on the verge of tears. I couldn't imagine how exhausted she must be after the last few days, both mentally and physically.

Jessica and I exchanged a glance, trying to decide how much to tell Melinda. "I'm not quite sure what it's about," I finally said. "But how about you wrap up here, then we'll drive down to the station with you and sort all of this out." It wasn't an outright lie. Other than the basics, Sheriff Jackson hadn't told me any details about what he was thinking with regard to Dario's guilt.

"What would I do without you, Tawny?" Melinda took my hands and shook them in thanks. "I'll just tell the house staff to wrap everything up and I'll get my purse." She looked around to find someone who worked at the house, and spotted the gardener attending to the flower arrangements at the front of the memorial.

I watched Melinda tell him something and he nodded, then went back to work taking down the memorial. "Okay. Our gardener Peter Flowers volunteered to take care of letting everyone know what to do. He's pretty torn up, poor guy. I think he worked for my aunt longer than anyone else who's here."

"I hope you don't mind me saying this, but I did notice a lot of people weren't that teary," I said, trying to lead

Melinda to give us more info on the people who showed up.

"Yeah well, my aunt didn't have many people who were actually close to her. So I'm guessing most of them were casual acquaintances or have some sort of morbid curiosity," Melinda waved off the comment.

Just then, Lady Sinclair came running out of the house. "Tawny! Melinda! Jessica!" I found it hard not to laugh at how dramatic she was. It only took a few seconds for her to get to us. "What *was* all of that commotion in the house during the service?"

"Yeah, I meant to ask about that," Melinda agreed. "What was that?"

"Oh just some local woman who tried to steal a candlestick to sell for some extra money," Jessica answered.

"At a memorial?! How *uncouth*!" Lady Sinclair exclaimed.

"That's so sad. She must have been desperate," Melinda added, with all of the compassion that was missing from Lady Sinclair's reaction.

"It definitely seemed like she was," Jessica said.

"You'll have to give me her information and tell me what she tried to take. I'll drop by and give it to her later," Melinda said without a moment of hesitation. I was touched at how genuine and instant the reaction from her was. It definitely didn't seem like the way a greedy heiress would respond. "Lady Sinclair, we have to head to the station. Sheriff Jackson is holding Dario hostage for some bogus crime to defraud my aunt."

"Oh..." was all Lady Sinclair could say, but she shot me a knowing glance. "Yes, well, you better get on with that then. Good luck."

"Let's get going," Melinda led us to the driveway. "Would you mind if I catch a ride with you? I still don't really know my way around this town."

"Sure!" Jessica said, and I was once again so thankful we drove her car today instead of mine. There would be something so out of place at seeing both of these flawless women in Ole Reliable.

Chapter 31

Once we were in the car on the way to the station, I decided to ask a question that had been nagging at me for a while. "Melinda, I know your aunt and uncle didn't get along, but are you at all surprised he didn't show up today?" It had seemed so odd to me that Elise's husband hadn't even attended her memorial. I knew they were estranged, but still.

To my surprise, Melinda laughed. "Tawny, there aren't two people on Earth who care less about each other than my aunt and uncle. They didn't dislike each other, they just never really cared for each other either. It was a sort of arranged marriage."

"Those still happen?" Jessica asked from the driver seat.

"Back then when families wanted to consolidate wealth, it happened more than you would think," Melinda explained.

"Consolidate wealth? But I thought they had a prenup?" I asked.

"I guess it was a bit of a post-nup. I never knew all of the details but they both came from wealthy families so they had that money to get them started. Then they made some good business decisions early in their marriage and more than doubled their fortune. When they separated, they decided to split everything down the middle including their homes. Aunt Elise got the Shantytown estate and my uncle kept their house in the south of France," she elaborated. "I'm not sure what caused them to get a post-nup but I do know it's not-so-secret that my uncle is gay. That's why they never had children."

"Why not get a divorce then? That seems like a cleaner split than a lengthy separation," Jessica wondered.

"To be honest I'm not sure. Even though they weren't religious, I assume it has something to do with breaking that vow. They'd rather live separately than break a promise they made in a church," Melinda suggested. "They were pretty old fashioned in many ways."

"How curious," Jessica said and I hummed in agreement.

Before long we were at the station. There were a few more people here now than had been earlier in the day. Officer Futch was manning the phone at the front. I didn't even need to explain why we were there since Melinda's presence made it obvious. I also suspected Sheriff Jackson gave him the heads up that we might show up. "Go on into the observation room," he sighed. "They haven't started yet."

I led Melinda and Jessica into the small, dark room that I was becoming too familiar with. Sheriff Jackson was in the room looking at some papers and keeping an eye on Dario. From the other side of the glass, it was clear Dario seemed anxious, sitting there under the fluorescent lights. "Looks like you're just in time. I'm about to head in there," Sheriff Jackson said to us. Then he looked at Melinda, "I'm sorry you have to go through this so soon after losing your aunt. I'm sure it can't be easy."

"Whom you still haven't given me the body for, by the way," Melinda added, but then softened. "Just hurry up please. Dario and I haven't spent time together in weeks and I'd like to have a glass of wine and hang out with my boyfriend after the nightmare that this day has turned out to be."

Sheriff Jackson nodded his head in agreement, but gave me a quick, knowing look. This would not be as painless for Melinda as she seemed to hope it would.

Chapter 32

As soon as Sheriff Jackson entered the interrogation room, Dario demanded to have a lawyer present before he answered any questions. "That is your right and we'll call a public defender down here for you if that's what you want. But in the meantime, let me tell you what we know. You don't have to say anything."

That quieted Dario down. From inside the observation room, we could all see Sheriff Jackson lay out a full table of papers. Unfortunately we couldn't see what they were exactly, but we could hear Sheriff Jackson explain them to Dario. "These are your phone, bank, and internet records, dating back to a few months before you met Melinda — we already got a warrant and checked this out. You can see from the bank records alone that we have proof of the Ponzi scheme you were involved in, and that you scammed other people in addition to Elise Huntington-Wilbury."

Dario's face went white, but Sheriff Jackson didn't give him the chance to say anything and continued on. "If you have a look at the phone records, you'll see that we can easily trace back to when you started talking to Ms. Huntington-Wilbury with regard to wiring Melinda's money, and then kept in touch long after. We've also tracked down 10 other numbers that go to similarly wealthy people. We've handed that over to Interpol, and once they finish their inquiries I'm sure they'll figure out your scam."

Dario looked worse by the second, but he stayed quiet. So Sheriff Jackson continued. "We also learned that you used the money you received to set up a private bank, or at least that's what you were telling these *'investors,'* but that never got off the ground, did it?"

"You don't know anything," Dario feebly broke his own silence.

Sheriff Jackson ignored the comment. "Like I said, I've already turned all of this over to Interpol so I'm not concerned with the schemes. I'm concerned with why you murdered Ms. Huntington-Wilbury."

"I didn't!" Dario shouted in defense. "How could I have? I wasn't even here!"

I watched poor Melinda's face fall with every new piece of paper further proving what Sheriff Jackson was saying.

Once he'd finished laying out the evidence, Sheriff Jackson said, "This last piece of paper right here shows that you and Ms. Huntington-Wilbury had a call about a week ago where she said she wanted to take her money out of the bank and that through the grapevine she'd discovered your scam. You also knew Melinda would inherit everything, and then you could get even more money out of her if her aunt was out of the way. That gives you a motive. Obviously you have access to money so you could have hired someone to do the job for you. That gives you the means to kill her."

"You can't possibly be able to prove what was said on that call. For all you know, Ms. Huntington-Wilbury was saying she was very pleased with her investment returns," Dario countered, breaking his silence again.

"Actually, I can. A few of the house staff members overheard the call. Apparently it was very odd for Ms. Huntington-Wilbury to raise her voice so this call was memorable to everyone who was within earshot," Sheriff Jackson said, then stopped talking, letting the room fall quiet again. It stayed like that for an uncomfortable amount of time. Even the three of us in the observation room didn't make a peep.

Finally, Dario spoke in a more pleading tone. "Okay you know what, fine. Yes, all of that is true, but I didn't kill her. Or have her killed, as you're insinuating. My relationship with Melinda is the real thing. I'll admit, when Melinda first came to the bank, I did see dollar signs. But then I got to know her, and now we're in love. I wouldn't jeopardize that," he said but was unconvincing.

Melinda was silently crying next to me. "Do you want to leave?" I asked her, but Melinda shook her head no.

"I want to hear the rest of it since he thinks I'm not here," she sniffled. "Who knows what'll come out of his mouth next." I nodded and we turned our attention back to the observation room.

"You've lied to me so your words have little meaning, Mr. Schmid. Now I can't simply *trust* that you're telling the truth," Sheriff Jackson said.

"But I *am*," Dario insisted. "How can I prove it to you?"

"That's up to you to figure out," Sheriff Jackson explained. Then he slowly gathered the stacks of papers he'd laid out on the table, putting them back into one big stack. I knew he was taking his time to give Dario a longer opportunity to talk, but Dario didn't. So Sheriff Jackson got up to leave the room, saying, "I'm going to go have a chat with Melinda. Maybe she can help you figure something out."

"No! Melinda can't know any of this," Dario insisted with urgency in his voice.

"Oh, she knows everything. She's on the other side of the one-way mirror. She got to the station right before I walked in here," Sheriff Jackson said in his usual cool, even tone.

Dario leapt to his feet and frantically ran over to the glass and pounded on it. "Melinda! I'm so sorry. I promise I had nothing to do with your aunt dying though. You have to believe me," he pleaded.

On our side of the mirror, Melinda stepped backwards until her back was pressed against the wall opposite the glass.

She was now audibly crying and my heart broke for her. "C'mon Melinda, I think you should go now," I said, looking at Jessica and nodding my head towards the door. This time, Melinda agreed and we all left the observation room.

As we did, Sheriff Jackson was securing the door to the interview room, but Dario caught a glimpse of us from the crack between the door and the door jamb before it was closed.

"Melinda!" he wailed, but it was cut off by the door clanking shut.

Melinda covered her face and ran out the front of the station to the car. Jessica chased after her, and I gave a wave to Sheriff Jackson before following them.

Chapter 33

Aside from Melinda thanking us for driving her to the station and apologizing for taking up so much of our time, there was little conversation on the drive back to the Huntington-Wilbury estate. Jessica and I reassured her that it was no big deal to drive her and offered to stay for a little while if she wanted company. Melinda insisted that all she wanted was to go inside, take a long bath, and to go to bed.

"Well that was pretty brutal," Jessica said after Melinda waved goodbye and closed her massive front door. "Do you really think she could be that naive?"

I thought back to my chat with Melinda when she admitted to not having that many friends, and how she hadn't suspected for a second that I was recording our conversation when I was asking questions about Dario. "Yeah, odd as it is, I really think she didn't have a clue. She just wanted someone to love her."

We were quiet for a few more minutes when my phone rang. It was Sheriff Jackson. I answered and Jessica whispered to put it on speakerphone so I did.

"You're on speakerphone," I said.

"Am I? With who else?" he asked with a curious tone, not a harsh one.

"Hiiii. It's me, Jessica. Your friendly neighborhood wrestler," she joked.

"Hello, Ms. Harrington. Well, I supposed you're involved in all of this now so you can hear the latest too," he started. "I've turned over all of my info on Dario to Interpol. This is an international thing and I don't want any part of that headache. I only brought him in to rattle his cage and confirm he wasn't the guy we were looking for. It's unfortunate Ms. Wilbury had to hear that though. Is she okay?"

"Eh, she will be. And it's better that she heard it straight from Dario instead of someone telling her. At least she won't think anyone was lying to her," I explained. "But how can you be so sure that Dario had nothing to do with it? You had a good point that it would be easy enough for him to hire a hit man. And he had means and motive."

"Exactly, and a hitman wouldn't have been this sloppy. It's all too much of a mess for me to believe any kind of professional was involved."

"So what's the next step?" I asked.

"Scott is still our strongest suspect, though it's looking more and more like he was set up. Might still bring him in again. He gives up more and more information every time we talk, even with his lawyer in the room" Sheriff Jackson said. "For now, I'm just going to go over the evidence again and sleep on it. Wanted to call and tell you that you should do the same."

"Okay, thanks for letting me know," I said and hung up the phone.

"If it wasn't Dario or Scott, and your gut says it wasn't Melinda, then who the heck could it be?" Jessica blurted.

"I really have no clue," I shrugged.

Chapter 34

When we got to Jessica's house, I went inside to change back into the clothes I'd arrived in, then said a quick goodbye before I got in my car and drove home.

I was lost in thought, running over all of the details of the case, when a reminder went off on my phone. I had a training session with Lady Sinclair the next morning.

As soon as I pulled up to the studio, I sent her a confirmation text to make sure she was still coming. Lady Sinclair answered almost immediately, confirming the appointment, and saying she couldn't wait to talk about what happened today.

Whenever Lady Sinclair said something like that, it meant that she had something new she wanted to share. So I felt hopeful that the morning session would produce some kind of new information; maybe some fresh perspective. To ensure that we had some time to chat, I intentionally extended my session with Lady Sinclair in my calendar. We'd have a bit of a longer warm up than usual, and to make sure the moves weren't so strenuous that they didn't leave her too winded to keep her from talking.

The next day, I stuck to my routine and got up early to go for a run before the session, returning with just enough time to set up. I got out a mat and a few lighter dumbbells, then did some cooldown stretches of my own while I waited for Lady Sinclair to arrive.

As usual, Lady Sinclair was wearing her oversized sunglasses and matching coat, always trying to seem incognito even though there was never any paparazzi looking for her.

"Nice to see you, Lady Sinclair," I took her jacket and hung it up like I always did, careful to put it on a thick wooden clothes hanger so it didn't break my flimsy plastic ones.

"We've seen quite a lot of each other lately, Tawny. Haven't we?" Lady Sinclair asked.

"We have. And I'm enjoying it," I smiled, hoping she didn't realize I was trying to butter her up.

"Me too darling, but maybe let's not make it quite so much of a habit. Ever since I pulled you in to help investigate poor Elise's murder things have been so *stressful* for me."

"Same here! Hopefully we can destress in the session today. I've got some light weights work," I offered. But then again, that was just how Lady Sinclair was.

"Perfect," Lady Sinclair said, gracefully sitting down onto the mat and beginning to stretch. "You have to tell me what happened at the memorial yesterday. We all heard a terrible crash and then never saw what came of it."

Since I'd only given her a brief explanation at the memorial, I filled her in on the details of Jane Goodall trying to steal the candlestick and Jessica tackling her.

Lady Sinclair was aghast. "My God! You think a town is safe and then something like that happens."

"Well, I do think it was a one-time thing. I wouldn't be too worried," I tried to reassure her. "But unfortunately, it does mean we're out of suspects." I hoped this would make Lady Sinclair give me some more information, anything, to help figure out what the next step in the investigation would be.

"Oh? I thought the sheriff was looking at Scott as one of the main suspects?" Lady Sinclair raised an eyebrow.

"He was, but that's a dead end without more evidence. I think he's going to question Scott again and see if there's anything else he's holding back. What he has now is not enough to go on though," I explained.

Lady Sinclair was quiet for a moment. Following my private investigator instincts, I prompted, "You don't think that there's something else he's not telling us, do you?"

"Well," Lady Sinclair sighed. "I wasn't going to tell you this because it's really none of my business..."

I had to hold back a smile because the majority of things Lady Sinclair talked about were really none of her business.

"The last time Scott and I met up, he told me about something a little troubling," Lady Sinclair went on. This time I was quiet in the hopes she'd fill the silence. It worked. "He told me about a book offer he'd gotten. A tell-all book."

Now it was Lady Sinclair's turn to be quiet. Over time I learned that she loved being asked to tell a story and frequently created these dramatic pauses, as though someone had written them into a script.

I gasped and played along. "A tell-all book? About what?" I asked.

"About Elise, if you can believe it. Apparently some publisher got word of her annual tea parties and wanted to write a book about it. Of course, Scott would need to hire a ghostwriter but he would be the one telling the story," Lady Sinclair spilled. "He said he was supposed to meet with the ghostwriter this week and get started. They wanted to know *everything* about Elise since so little was known publicly about her."

An offer like this tell-all this wasn't too shocking. The public loved books about obscure yet interesting figures. Elise Huntinton-Wilbury certainly fit that bill. "Didn't Scott have to sign a non-disclosure agreement when he started working at the estate?" I asked. When people worked for wealthy employers, they typically had to sign one of these documents — more commonly called an NDA. It was to protect them from situations exactly like the one that Scott had been offered.

"Unfortunately for Elise, no. She didn't make her staff sign NDAs. She never got used to the modern world, and refused to believe the idea that people would try to make money by selling people's secrets. But don't worry, I've already had a little chat with Melinda to let her know that if she intends to keep the staff on, she needs them to sign NDAs," Lady Sinclair reassured me. But Melinda's handling of the estate was the furthest thing from my mind.

"That's very smart of you," I played along.

"Yes, well, we *all* have to look out for each other, don't we," Lady Sinclair said it like she was doing everyone a favor by telling Melinda this one piece of advice. "Anyways, I told Scott it was a tacky thing to do. I mean, of course it's morally wrong to turn over someone's private life like that, but it's also tacky. And that's almost worse if you ask me," she looked to me to see if I agreed. I nodded my head to show that I did, trying to keep her talking. "I have no idea if he went through with it. We didn't really have *that* kind of relationship, you know."

"I wonder if he did. That would certainly be reason enough to put him back on the suspect list. Are you still in contact with him?" I was unsure if the question was taking our tenuous friendship a step too far.

"Good God, no. I'm already embarrassed enough that half the town knows we were... together. I don't need the gossips to think there's actually something long term there," she seemed a little disgusted at the prospect. I had to stifle a laugh because she was the queen of "the gossips."

We finished up the session with little other new information surfacing, but that was okay. This was a pretty big detail that I couldn't wait to tell Sheriff Jackson when we were done.

As soon as Lady Sinclair drove away, I picked up the phone and dialed the number to the station.

Officer Futch answered the phone. "Shantytown Sheriff's Station," his tone was flat.

"Hi, is this Officer Futch?" I asked, hoping that identifying him by name would make him feel important and get him to warm up to me.

"Speaking," he answered.

"I thought it sounded like you. Hi, this is Tawny Monroe," I tried to sound cheerful, but I could already feel Officer Futch's demeanor change through the phone.

"Probably sounded like me because it is me," he snapped. "Is this a personal call, Ms. Monroe? Because we've got an investigation going on, and I can't have this line tied up for too long."

I realized how frustrated he was, but had to hold back a laugh at how folksy that entire phrase sounded. It was the 2020s. Even a semi-rural Sheriff's Station had to have call waiting and likely more than one phone line. There were kids in high school who wouldn't even have the slightest clue what he was talking about.

I took a deep breath and wiped the smile off my face. "Well I definitely don't want to do that. But yes, I am looking for the sheriff. Not to say hi though. I have some new information. Is he there right now?"

There was a beat of silence on the other line. "How'd you get new information?"

Hadn't Officer Futch caught on by now that I was 'officially' helping in the investigation? "I have my sources,"

I said, no longer amused with this conversation. "Is he there?"

"Hold on one second," the officer said.

I waited for what seemed like forever until Sheriff Jackson's warm, calming voice came over the other end. "Sheriff Jackson, who am I speaking with?"

"Hi!" I said too enthusiastically.

"Tawny, hi. Futch didn't say it was you. Futch, why didn't you tell me it was Tawny?" She heard him ask the officer.

The phone caught the far off response, "Didn't think it mattered."

"Well, I suppose it doesn't really," Sheriff Jackson replied and my heart sank a little. I could have sworn that he'd sounded happy to hear my voice on the other end of the phone, but maybe that was all in my head. I tried to remind myself to stay focused on the task at hand. "What's up, Monroe?"

"I've got some new information that could point to a real reason why Scott is our main suspect again," I said with renewed enthusiasm at the prospect of solving this case.

"Oh? What's that?" he asked.

"I just came from a session with Lady Sinclair. She said during one of her, uh, *encounters* with Scott, he mentioned that a publisher had approached him to write a tell-all book about Elise Huntington-Wilbury," I explained.

"A tell-all book? Would he legally be able to do that?" Sheriff Jackson wondered.

"I had the same question, and I'm not positive he could. But Lady Sinclair said that Ms. Huntington-Wilbury didn't have her staff sign a NDA, so it's possible." If I was being honest, I still had my doubts. Her estate could possibly come after him if they could prove that what he had to say was libel and could hurt her image posthumously.

"Do you think that's why he started having an affair with her?" Sheriff Jackson asked. "To get more information about Elise?"

It was a good theory, but the timelines didn't match up. "No, I think they were together a long time before he got the offer. But he could have used their relationship as a way to get *more* money out of the tell-all." Then I asked, "You can't really call it an affair if she and her husband were completely estranged, can you?"

"To be honest, I don't care what it's called. It's none of my business, unless it has to do with solving this murder," he said. "Okay so, the tell-all is Scott's motive. And I have to admit, it does look really suspicious that he didn't tell us about this earlier. Makes me wonder what else he's hiding."

"He's not a perfect suspect, but the motive and opportunity are there. The thing that still doesn't make sense to me is the weapon," I said more thinking out loud than telling him.

But Sheriff Jackson didn't realize I was talking to myself and responded, "Well, that's because the weapon was the concrete hitting her head when she fell. Whether she was pushed or not is the question," he replied.

"No, I know that. I mean the chlorine tablets. Why would Scott do that when he's the pool boy? It's not like he's some sort of sick serial killer who was leaving a calling card," I made sure to explain what I was thinking this time rather than letting him assume. "And surely he'd know that it would make him look like the prime suspect."

"Maybe he was just getting started in his life of crime but we stopped him," Sheriff Jackson offered, but I wasn't sure if it was a joke or not. When I didn't say anything he confirmed that he was kidding. "Lighten up, Monroe. It's a joke. I don't actually think he's a budding serial killer."

"Oh, oh yeah I knew that," I tried to play it cool.

"Anyways, this is a great new lead. Thanks for bringing it to me. I'll go see if I can find Scott and question him again. Maybe for good this time. Talk to you later, Tawny," Sheriff Jackson said and hung up before I had a chance to say anything else.

The abrupt end to the call made me feel a little taken aback. I hoped it was just him wanting to get to Scott sooner than later and not an indication of anything else, like a waning interest in talking to me. It was at this moment I finally acknowledged to myself that I had a full blown crush on the Sheriff, and resolved to talk myself out of it.

I knew how dangerous the life of a private investigator could be, let alone the life of a Sheriff. Did I really want to get involved with a man who I'd be worrying about where he was all of the time? Then again, it wasn't like dangerous crime was an issue in Shantytown.

At that point, I stopped my internal monologue and said out loud to myself, "Enough!" I realized I had gone from 0 to 60 in my mind and was already starting to plan a future with Sheriff Jackson, a man I barely knew at all. Resolving to focus on the case at hand, I did what I always did when something was on my mind. I went to DINE.

Chapter 35

There was nothing quite like DINE's chef Ferdinand's truffle fries and Sandi's good company to help lift whatever boulder was on my mind on any given day.

When I pulled Ole Reliable into the lot, I noticed the only other car there was a brand new purple Porsche SUV. Some people might have felt self conscious parking next to a car worth 10x more than their own, but that was just part of living in Shantytown. If I let that get to me, I'd never be able to park anywhere. Besides, everyone here was more or less the same, no matter what their bank account statements said.

I saw Sandi right away when I walked in. She was at the bar pouring coffee for the couple who had just sat down. "Hi Tawny, your booth is open," she said, pointing to the booth that Sheriff Jackson and I had sat in with her the night of the murder.

This phrase was a code from Sandi. Whenever she had something important to tell me, she'd say to take the booth. Since Sandi only shared secrets when it was necessary for one reason or another, it was rare for her to say this line. Typically when I came in for a chat, I'd sit at the bar where the couple was now seated and I'd catch up with both Sandi and Ferdinand. But this time, Sandi had something she didn't want Ferdinand to hear.

Sitting in the booth, I took a minute to exhale and relax. I may be a personal trainer, but I often found myself forgetting some of the advice I gave my own students. Closing my eyes, I released the tension in my jaw and shoulders, took a deep inhale for four seconds, then held it for two, and exhaled out of my mouth for eight seconds. I immediately felt the stress I'd been holding leave my body, and I opened my eyes.

I jumped at the sight of Sandi sitting across from me, staring back and smiling. "Oh! I thought I'd hear you sit down before I saw you!"

"Don't mind me," Sandi said. "You looked so relaxed I didn't want to disturb you. Matter of fact, let me do one of those breaths with you." So we both joined in on a few more deep breaths. "Man, I feel so relaxed I could take a nap now," Sandi laid her head on the table and made a fake snoring sound. "Ahhh, I'm just pulling your leg."

I couldn't help but laugh. Sandi always put me in a good mood, and the deep breathing had helped me feel more clear than I'd felt in hours, maybe days.

"So what brings you here today? I doubt it's just the food," Sandi said.

"Well, it's definitely the food, but I also need some advice," I admitted.

"What's up, buttercup?" Sandi loved using old timey sayings.

"You know I'm helping with this case, and we're kind of out of leads," I started explaining. I recapped how the investigation had been going so far, and all of the dead ends we'd hit. I even told Sandi about Jessica tackling Jane Goodall at the memorial.

"Jane told me all about it," Sandi said.

"So you know her?" I perked up, remembering Melinda said she wanted to help the woman out if we found her. Maybe Sandi would know where she lived. And that would give me another excuse to check in on Melinda, aka snoop around.

"Yeah, she's lived here just about as long as I have. Poor woman seems snakebitten. Nothing ever goes right for her. When she has trouble making rent, I pay her to come in and deep clean the restaurant on the weekends," Sandi explained.

"I'll have to get you in touch with Melinda. After she heard why Jane was taking the silver candlestick she said she wanted to give it to her if it would help with the bills," I explained.

Sandi put her hand on her chin like she was thinking. "I don't know this Melinda very well, but she seems a heckuvalot more human than her aunt was. You think she'll stick around after everything settles down?"

"I honestly have no clue, but I agree. I hope she does," and it was the truth. Melinda was starting to grow on me.

"Okay well back to the clues. This is fun, like solving a riddle," Sandi leaned in when she said it, like we were sharing secrets.

I finished filling her in and she was quiet. Finally Sandi said, "I debated whether I should tell you this or not, but I had a feeling it would be useful to you. That's why I sent you over to this booth. I heard through the grapevine that Elise Huntington-Wilbury was also in a relationship with the gardener Peter Flowers."

"What?!" I was shocked this hadn't come up in my talks with Lady Sinclair. Maybe Elise had been a master at hiding her little trysts. "How do you know that's true?"

"You know I'm not going to reveal my sources, honey. But I can say with certainty that it's true," Sandi assured me. "Apparently they had been together for a long time;

way before the poolboy Scott worked there. Maybe even before he was born to be honest with you. I'm not sure exactly how long, but safe to say it was a long-term thing."

"I'm surprised no one mentioned this when Sheriff Jackson and his people interviewed the staff," I mused.

"I'll say this for my source, it took about half a bottle of whiskey to let even this little bit slip. So I don't think some cursory questioning would do the trick," Sandi explained, then got up to check on the other couple who was at the bar. "Hope that helps, hon," she said as she walked away.

Suddenly I was no longer in the mood for food. I had to get in touch with Sheriff Jackson again. Scott could still be guilty of being a sleazeball, but now we had a lead on someone else who could be the killer. Or who could have been the one to frame him. If Peter thought that Scott was also sleeping with Elise, then he might have killed her in a rage and framed Scott.

But why would he kill Elise and not Scott? Seems the more likely thing would be for Peter to kill Scott and get him out of the picture so he could be with Elise again. I knew from past experience that everyone could act out of character when emotions were high.

I got up and left DINE, waving and thanking Sandi on my way out, then hurried back to my studio. I had an afternoon aerial yoga session with Jessica, which is why we were having it at the studio instead of up at Jessica's mansion. It would be too much work to get the hammocks set up at her place.

At the studio, I'd installed hooks in the ceiling precisely for this purpose. I grabbed a stepstool and hooked up the hammocks we'd be using then waited for my friend to get there.

The first time I tried aerial yoga, I thought it would just be something fun to try but not too challenging. I couldn't have been more wrong. Aerial yoga took yoga on the ground to the next level in terms of coordination and strength. At the beginning, even though the hammocks felt silky, they could dig right into the thigh if all the muscles weren't activated, making holding poses pretty intense.

Realizing I'd forgotten to actually eat while I was at DINE, I took a big bite of a protein bar when Jessica walked in right on time. "Hi!" she said in her usual cheerful self. I sped up my chewing, holding up one finger to indicate I'd be with Jessica in a second as soon as my mouth wasn't full, which made the movie star laugh.

"Wow, that's embarrassing," I said once I swallowed and was able to talk again.

"I'll say," Jessica joked. "Skip lunch?"

"You know me well," I said. "Let's get to this workout because I need to pick your brain about some stuff when we're done."

"About the case?" Jessica couldn't hide the excitement in her voice.

"Yes, I think we have a new lead," I nodded.

"Oh! Yeah, let's get this session over with then tell me. If we start talking now, we'll never get to the workout and I leave to go back to L.A. tonight," Jessica explained while walking over to the hammocks and climbing in.

Chapter 36

An hour later, we each laid upside down in our respective hammocks and discussed the case. Jessica read somewhere that laying upside down reversed the blood flow, giving the brain even more oxygen. "It'll help us think better!" she announced when I gave her a quizzical look. She insisted it was how she memorized some of her longer monologues. I filled her in on all of the things I'd learned since we'd last talked and what Sandi had told me.

"I think we should storyboard this," Jessica said, popping out of her hammock and going to the front desk. She pulled out some post-it notes, two pens, and went back to the open floor space.

We made notes for each of the suspects, jotting down details about each of them. Like, "Scott: poolboy, in a relationship with Lady Sinclair and with Elise, writing a tell-all, not very smart." Then we both started trying to make connections between people. We didn't have a pinboard and thumbtacks around, so we laid out our notes on the floor, using tools like jump ropes and yoga straps to draw the lines.

Once we were done, we had a bit of a clearer picture of what was going on, but not by much. "Tawny, I hate to say this, but it still looks like it's either Scott or Peter the gardener," Jessica resolved.

"It really does look like that, doesn't it?" I agreed. "If you had to make an arrest right now, who would it be?"

Jessica was quiet for a moment then said, "I'd have to say Scott. This whole tell-all thing makes him look really bad. Especially since he's been so secretive about it"

"What about the chlorine?" That's the piece that's not fitting for me."

"I think he *tried* to poison her, but it didn't work. I think she spit it out," Jessica explained. "Maybe that was when she fell."

"That's definitely plausible, and still the strongest theory we have," I agreed. "Okay, I'm going to call Sheriff Jackson."

I picked up my cell and called the station.

"Sheriff's Station," the familiar voice of Officer Futch came across the line.

"Hi, Officer Futch," I was less cheerful than before. Why did I care so much about this guy liking me anyway? I had a crush on the sheriff, not him.

Futch sighed on the other end. "Sheriff Jackson isn't here right now, Tawny."

I had to admit to myself that I was a little surprised he recognized my voice. "Oh, um, okay do you know how I can reach him?"

"He's got his cell. You can try that," he offered.

I thought about it and at first wasn't sure if I had Sheriff Jackson's phone number, but then remembered he'd contacted me before. So I just had to look back through my phone.

"He's out trying to bring in Scott. We were having a little trouble locating him so the Sheriff decided to go out on his own and find him."

"Huh, that's interesting," I said.

Futch seized on my words. "Why?! What did you figure out? If you know something, you have a legal obligation to tell us," the words spilled out of him. He was so loud that Jessica could hear him even though I wasn't on speakerphone. She rolled her eyes and I had to try hard not to laugh.

"No she doesn't, *Futch*" Jessica said, but the man on the other end didn't seem to hear her.

"We're still not sure of anything. Just thinking about some theories, but Scott looks like the most likely suspect,"

I said, trying to calm him down. "I'll just call the sheriff and see if he picks up," I ended the call.

He picked up on the second ring. "Sheriff Jackson," he answered.

"Hi, it's Tawny," I put on my most business-y voice possible. There was no flirting here. "I got a new piece of evidence, so Jessica and I were going over everything again. But we're still sure Scott is your guy."

"I'm pretty sure of it too, though I'd like to hear about this new evidence," Sheriff Jackson said with his classic, cool voice.

"Well, it's not really important anymore, but I found out that Elise had a relationship with the gardener, Peter Flowers. Potentially a long-term one. But I still think it's more likely that Scott's our guy," I said with confidence. "Jessica and I talked it over and we think that the chlorine residual was from Scott trying to force her to swallow a tablet and that's how the scuffle ensued. Then she fell, hitting her head."

Sheriff Jackson was quiet for a beat, taking in the new information. "I think it's Scott too, but not because of that. Although that's good thinking. Currently, I think it's him because I can't find him *anywhere*," he said and it was the first time I'd heard him with any kind of frustration in his voice, even though it was only a hint.

Just then, outside the window of the studio, I heard a loud truck rumble by. I got a peek at it just long enough to see that it was the same work truck from the Huntington-Wilbury estate. It had to be Scott.

"I think I found him!" I said too-loudly and motioned for Jessica to look. She was back in the hammock hanging upside down and nearly fell out trying to twist around and see what I was pointing at. Then I remembered Jessica hadn't been at the party so she hadn't seen the truck. "Scott's truck just went flying by my studio," I explained to both Jessica and Sheriff Jackson.

"Which way was he going?" Sheriff Jackson asked, losing most of the cool in his voice, instead sounding tense.

"Hard to say, but I know it's the direction I would go if I was heading up to the estate," I said, already pulling on my sneakers and motioning for Jessica to hurry up with her own.

"I'm on my way. Don't go up there, Tawny. It could be dangerous," Sheriff Jackson warned.

I didn't want to get into it with him, so I simply hung up the phone. He called back right away, but I hit ignore. There was no talking me out of going up there. I knew that the studio was close to the bottom of the hill, so if I was right and that was Scott driving the truck, Jessica and

I could drive there faster than the Sheriff. We got into my old black sedan and started towards the estate.

Chapter 37

By this time, I was getting pretty tired of the twisty-turny ride up to the estate and was looking forward to when this was solved so I wouldn't have to go up there anymore. On the bright side, this time I didn't have to worry about GPS because Jessica knew the roads in these hills like the back of her hand and guided me with ease. That didn't make the drive any easier on my car though. Just one more time, I told myself as I tried to whip Ole Reliable around the curves.

After a few corners, Jessica, who was a pretty fast driver herself, said, "Uh, hey Tawny, I'd like to get there in one piece." I looked over and saw my friend holding on to the bar above the door for dear life. I laughed and slowed down a little bit. Jessica slowly let go of the bar and settled back in. Now driving at the legal speed limit, I had the chance to take in how the weather changed as we made our way up the hill. Down in the town it had been sunny and about 70 degrees; the usual perfect Shantytown weather. But as we climbed, a foggy mist settled in. It wasn't so dense that it was hard to see the road, but it was thick enough to give the rest of the drive a bit of an eerie feeling.

What was a short time later — but probably felt like an eternity for Jessica based on how pale her face was getting — we arrived at the gate which was still wide open, then quietly pulled into the driveway. I noticed no other cars were here and wondered where Melinda had parked, or if she was home at all. Everything looked much different than the last time I was up here for the memorial. All of the hustle and bustle of the vendors tearing down then setting up an event was gone, let alone the ambience of the events themselves.

I couldn't help but think it made the place look less impressive and *more* haunted. The fog only added to the intimidation factor, too. I started wondering what it must have been like to be Ms. Huntington-Wilbury, up here all alone for the most part. It was probably pretty depressing. I couldn't fault her for looking for companionship wherever she could find it.

We got out of the car, quietly closing our doors so that if anyone was around, hopefully they wouldn't hear.

Jessica snapped me out of my thoughts with a terse whisper. "Tawny!" I looked to my right and saw that Jessica had lost no time moving further into the premises. She'd already crept to the side of the house and was waving her arm frantically in a circular motion to try and hurry me over, which I did, quickly tiptoeing.

As I got closer to Jessica I could hear why she had so much urgency. There were voices somewhere in the distance. They were too far away to tell who they were and what they were saying, but it was clear there were two people talking loud enough for the sound to carry over to us.

"Which way should we go?" Jessica asked. We looked out at the vast lawn in front of us. There was only about 10 feet of visibility so things went from looking haunted to being downright eerie.

Jessica had been up here for parties before, but not me, and without either a party or a memorial taking up the space, it looked bigger than I could have imagined. The maze hedges bordered the right and back sides of the lawn with a few openings to enter. To the left I could barely make out the road that led down to the staff parking lot.

"I honestly have no clue which direction the voices were in," I said, looking from one side to the other. I tried to think it over: if we went to the right through the maze, there was a good chance we'd get lost. Forget finding the owners of the voices we were hearing, we might not find our own way out. Then we'd really be in trouble. If we went down the staff road to the left, we would be exposed and risked being seen. If only it was clearer where the voices were drifting from.

But that didn't matter because our decision was post-poned by another sound. I heard a car come up the drive-way. I couldn't see who it was because of the thick marine layer. Maybe that meant they couldn't see us standing out here in the middle of the field either. It sounded like it came to a stop behind where I thought I'd parked my car.

Chapter 38

"What should we do?" I whispered to Jessica. There was nowhere to hide, and the footsteps from the driver sounded like they were walking our way.

Jessica shrugged, looking just as unsure as I was. Then through the fog a figure started to form. At first I thought it was Melinda or Dario. I prayed it wasn't the latter, but if he started a fight, the two of us could probably take him.

The figure continued to materialize, and there was the strong silhouette of Sheriff Jackson heading our way. "I thought I told you —" he started to say, but Jessica and I waved our hands and she put a finger to her lips indicating for him to stop talking. So he did, and he moved closer towards us.

It looked like he was going to ask a question, but as he was opening his mouth to do so, the sounds of the voices grew louder. These two people were now clearly shouting. Sheriff Jackson lifted his head to listen.

"We were trying to figure out which way they were coming from when you pulled up," I whispered.

Thankfully the raised tone made it clear which direction we had to go: toward the maze. The fog in the entrance made it look ominous. Guess we have to go in there," Jessica shrugged and started to run on her tiptoes towards the nearest opening in the hedge. It made her look like a ballerina. Meanwhile I was pretty sure I looked like a villain from a cartoon. I followed her lead anyway and looked back to see that Sheriff Jackson was coming too. Unfortunately he wasn't tiptoeing, which made me feel silly for doing so.

Once inside the maze, I was transported back to a few days ago during the party when I'd been here for the first time. I felt completely lost in here now just like before, but I followed Jessica who somehow seemed to know where she was going.

The voices were growing steadily louder, and I knew we were on the right track. We still couldn't make out the words but the tones sounded angry, deep, and masculine. Thinking back to the night of the tea party, I remembered how the hedges muffled specific sounds and figured we wouldn't be able to hear their actual words until we were right up on the people. I felt like we were almost to the owners of the voices until we hit a fork in the maze. Jessica stopped.

"Which way?" I whispered.

"I'm not sure," Jessica said, looking between the two paths.

They seemed identical to me, except for the fact that one went straight and the other turned to the left. "I thought you knew where you were going?" I asked, now starting to panic that we might not only lose the two men but also that we might be lost in general.

"That's what I thought, too," Sheriff Jackson said, but his voice was a little too loud and both of us shushed him. He was cowed back into silence. We listened to see if the voices had stopped, indicating that they'd heard the three of us talking, but they were just as strong as before; maybe even a little stronger now.

After a few tense moments, Jessica whispered, "This way!" and took off to the left.

"Are you sure?" I asked, suspicious of how Jessica suddenly knew the right way to go when she had no clue only seconds ago.

"Do you have a better idea?" Jessica asked, dripping with snark.

Sheriff Jackson and I swapped a look, shrugged our shoulders, then kept on going. It seemed like the deeper we got into the maze the more forks there were. Jessica was so light and graceful that she nearly floated ahead of us but I couldn't tell her to slow down without being too loud. So Sheriff Jackson and I just rushed to keep up.

Then I heard a thunk behind me and turned to see that Sheriff Jackson had tripped over a low hanging branch that had grown too far from the hedge.

"Are you okay?" I quietly asked, going back to help him up, but he was already on his feet, brushing himself off.

"Nothing's hurt but my pride," he smiled and for the first time ever I thought I saw him blush.

The incident took only seconds but in that short amount of time, Jessica had managed to disappear from our sight.

Chapter 39

"Oh no," I said to myself out loud. Sheriff Jackson was quiet, listening to the voices. They were the loudest and strongest they'd been yet. I realized one of them sounded familiar. "Is that Scott?!" I asked, keeping my voice low even though I was excited. The sound drifting towards us definitely sounded like Scott's usual bored, whiny tone, like he was too cool for whatever conversation he was currently involved in.

The sheriff was quiet for another few moments before saying, "I can't be sure but it would make sense if it was. Let's go this way." He moved ahead of me and began leading the way. My sense of direction was never the greatest so I was happy to follow behind. Besides, the view ack here wasn't that bad either. From what I could see, Sheriff Jackson did not skip leg day at the gym.

A few more turns through the maze and we could finally hear what the two people were saying, but there was no sign of Jessica. Sheriff Jackson slowed his pace and we began slowly creeping towards them. I was thankful that it gave me a chance to catch my breath. I'd been breathing so hard that I was scared it would give us away. "I'm certain that's Scott," I told Sheriff Jackson and he nodded in agreement. "But who is the other person?" Sheriff Jackson shrugged, also unsure. I'd talked to a lot of people over the past few days, but the voice didn't sound familiar at all.

The hedges were too dense to see through but it was clear there was an opening up ahead. That meant we were right on the other side of the hedge from Scott and whoever it was that he was talking to. We pressed our ears to the hedge to hear better, like we were trying to listen through a wall.

I realized my head was tilted to the left, while Sheriff Jackson's was tilted to the right, leaving me and the Sheriff staring right at each other. It was a little intense and I considered turning the other way, but figured it would be more awkward if I turned my head the other way at this point.

We were so close to each other that I could smell wintergreen gum on his breath and I suddenly felt self-conscious about what my own might smell like.

"You set me up! Admit it!" The voice that we were sure was Scott said to the other person.

"I didn't and even if I did, you can't prove it!" The other voice said. It sounded older and deeper than Scott's, but a tone of voice could give the wrong impression of what people looked like more often than not, especially in a town full of actors.

I exchanged questioning looks with Sheriff Jackson to see if he could tell who the other voice was but he just shook his head. Then he motioned for me to move closer to the opening in the hedge. We inched our way there as quietly as possible.

"I'm leaving and going down to town to tell Sheriff Jackson that it was you. Once my lawyer found out about the chlorine tablets, I knew it had to be your sloppy work," Scott said. "Judging by your reaction here today, I was right."

"For the millionth time, you have no proof! In fact, if you keep reminding them about the chlorine, that points to you even more," the other voice said.

Just then, I heard a sudden rustling in the hedge right behind me and nearly screamed when I saw a figure creeping up by my side. Luckily I noticed just in time that it was Jessica. I had to physically cover my mouth with my hands to keep from making a sound.

Jessica wasn't paying attention to me though. She was focused on pushing the branches of a balding spot in the hedge open a little more, trying to create a little peep hole. I nudged her, hoping she'd get the hint and be quiet. But Jessica waved me off and continued trying to push the branches around to make a hole. Sometimes she really got *too* into sleuthing.

Scott continued the conversation. "You're just a dumb, old man. You thought Elise loved you? I wasn't the only one she was fooling around with here."

"Shut up!" The other man sounded a little more on edge than before. "Don't you dare say that about her."

"Say what? The truth?" Scott laughed. "I'm serious. She got around. Why do you think she kept this place locked up so tight? It was like her own little harem. You were probably outside too much to notice."

My ears perked up at this bit of information. "Outside too much to notice" sounded a lot like it could be Peter Flowers, the gardener. So Sandi's theory may have been right after all.

"Why you piece of —" the older man cut himself off as he lunged at Scott. We weren't at the opening in the maze yet and couldn't see what was happening, but we could hear the scuffle. Jessica, however, stayed at her spot in the hedge, able to at least see *something*.

"What should we do?" Sheriff Jackson whispered to me while Jessica took the commotion as an opportunity to snap a few bigger branches and deepen her peephole. I rolled my eyes. She was definitely going to give us away. But her risky efforts paid off and the opening was fairly wide, but not quite deep enough to give us a clear view, only her. And her head had nearly disappeared into it.

Before I had a chance to answer the Sheriff's question, there was a yelp and a loud cracking sound next to me. I turned around and saw my theory was confirmed. Peter and Scott came crashing through the hedge where Jessica's peephole had weakened it. They tumbled on top of the actress.

Chapter 40

Instead of lying there waiting for the men to get up, Jessica sprang into action. She'd recently acted in a few action films and was training in all kinds of martial arts while in L.A. She usually had a stunt person do the most dangerous moves, but it was always important to her that she be able to do enough to make a scene look realistic.

So after she freed herself from the small dogpile, Jessica jumped back from the men, assuming a fighting stance, ready to strike. Peter was the one who fell closest to her, and Jessica wasted no time getting him into a headlock, applying pressure to the sides of his neck in what was commonly called "the sleeper hold." This would deprive his brain of oxygen so he'd start to pass out, but would protect his windpipe so he didn't suffocate.

I loved that my friend always found new ways to surprise me and I had to hold back a laugh at how adept she was with this move. But I reminded myself that now wasn't the time to be entertained and moved to help Peter out of the hold.

"No way," Jessica said to me, refusing to lighten her grip. "Either he tells us what happened or he's passing out and telling us at the station."

"He can't tell us if you don't let up," I reminded Jessica, who considered the advice for a couple of seconds then abruptly let Peter go. He collapsed and rolled off to the side, taking deep breaths and trying to get his bearings.

Meanwhile, Sheriff Jackson had easily apprehended Scott who tried to make a getaway. "Let me go, man. Didn't you hear any of that? I'm the wrong guy. This is police brutality!" He tried to shake loose of Sheriff Jackson's hold, which didn't look like it was taking too much effort out of the Sheriff, easily holding Scott's hands behind his back.

Peter finally sat up on his knees and after a few deep breaths looked like he was about to go after Scott again. Then to everyone's surprise, Peter collapsed and started sobbing. Uncontrollable, gasping sobs that made us all exchange glances, unsure if we should go over and comfort the man or not.

"Fine! I did it, okay?!" he finally blubbered. "I can't go on like this. She deserved better."

Sheriff Jackson let go of Scott's hands, and Scott pulled them to his chest, rubbing his wrists like he'd been hurt. "You're going to hear from my lawyer about this," he said but the Sheriff ignored him.

Jessica switched from assailant to comforter, kneeling next to Peter and putting her arm around him. He either didn't seem to notice or didn't care that she was the one who'd been choking him only seconds ago as he leaned into her shoulder and continued sobbing. She quietly patted his back and told him it was okay.

As sad as this was, we needed answers. I walked over and squatted down in front of Peter, nodding to Jessica to back off a little bit so he'd come back to the present.

"Peter, what do you mean 'she deserved better'?" I asked, hoping that talking about Elise rather than himself would get him to admit guilt faster. Jessica shot me a look as though asking what she should do. I shrugged, so Jessica kept lightly patting the man on the back.

"Oh, shut up, Peter. No wonder you weren't enough for Elise. Look at you!" Scott spat. This immediately stopped Peter's cries, rage welling up inside of him. I realized he was going to charge Scott and instinctually pushed him back down as he tried to stand up.

Unfortunately when I did that, we both ended up toppling onto Jessica. "Ouch, you guys! C'mon!" she squeaked as she tried to move out from beneath us, which wasn't easy because Peter was still trying to get to Scott.

Meanwhile, Sheriff Jackson didn't need to hold Scott back. The pool boy had no intention of hurting Peter with anything but words. He laughed as I kept Peter pinned away from him. Peter finally ran out of steam and fell limply on the ground.

I let him go and tried to talk to him again, hoping he'd be more open now that he was clearly wiped out physically and emotionally. I talked quietly, only to him, though everyone else was close enough to hear our conversation too. "Peter, what do you mean she deserved better?"

Peter sniffled and said just above a whisper, "I killed her. She deserved better than that."

I looked at Sheriff Jackson and we exchanged a knowing glance. We'd need far more than a simple admission of guilt, in order to convict him. People made admissions all of the time to try and take the fall for family members or spouses.

"I know it's hard, Peter, but you have to tell us exactly what happened," I urged him in the most gentle voice I could summon, but it was difficult because at this point I was getting frustrated. One way or another, he was going to have to tell us and all of this emotion was becoming a little too much.

Finally, Peter took a deep breath, exhaled, then started talking. "Last week I heard Scott telling Lady Sinclair about the tell-all book deal he was offered, to expose Elise's secrets, and the life she worked so hard to keep away from prying eyes." His voice was low and flat, almost like he was in a trance. "When Lady Sinclair said that he shouldn't do it, I knew he was still thinking about writing it because he told Leonardo Casa."

"The house manager?" Sheriff Jackson asked to confirm.

"Yes. Another scumbag," Peter said, shooting Scott a dirty look.

"Hey, I wasn't the creep listening to other people's conversations," Scott shot back.

"Anyways," Peter continued. "I heard Scott and Leonardo talking about the tell-all. Apparently..." Peter broke off and I worried he would fall apart again, but after a couple of deep, stabilizing breaths he continued on. "Apparently Leonardo had a relationship with Elise, too. But like Scott, he didn't care about *her*, only what she could offer him."

"Wait, she was paying you all to sleep with her?" Jessica interjected.

"Not exactly," Scott said. "As you know, that would be *illegal*," he put emphasis on the last word and stared at Sheriff Jackson. "Anyways, that's besides the point."

"Maybe not," Sheriff Jackson said, "But we'll determine that later. Go on, Peter."

"After I heard Leonardo and Scott talking, I decided to confront Elise. I wanted to ask her why she'd betrayed me like this. I wanted to ask why she was so trusting of people who clearly didn't care about her," he continued, back in his trance-like tone. "She was very busy with planning the party though and I didn't get the chance. Until I saw her in the maze just before it started. I was cleaning up the hedges in case anyone came this way. She was strolling by and saw me. She looked so beautiful," the waterworks sprung a leak again.

Everyone was losing their patience with Peter, especially Jessica. "Dude, she cheated on you and lied. C'mon, pull yourself together," she held him by the shoulders and gave him a little shake. "Take a deep breath in," they both made an inhale sound, "andddd exhale." They both exhaled.

Peter patted Jessica on the hand. "Thank you, that helped. I also want to say I loved your last movie."

"Thank you," Jessica gave him a warm smile. I always marveled at how Jessica seemed so gracious when she accepted compliments. It never seemed haughty. Capitalizing on their new camaraderie, Jessica said "Okay, Peter, you're almost done. Now finish telling us what happened."

Chapter 41

Peter nodded in agreement and exhaled again. "Anyways, she came in and started flirting with me. I was in no mood since she'd been ignoring me for days. I told her I knew about her and Scott, and Leonardo. Elise denied all of it. I'll admit, I was mad. I would never hurt her, not on purpose, but I had never been that angry before in my life. Eventually, she admitted she had relationships with them but said she only loved me. Then I told her about Scott's tell-all book, and she accused *me* of lying. She shoved me, and I tripped backwards. She tried to catch me, but both of us ended up falling. But when she fell, her head hit the edge of the fountain."

He started crying again, but Jessica caught his eye and they took a deep breath together. He continued, "I was obviously shocked. I tried to help her up, but she wasn't moving. There wasn't a lot of blood so I didn't think she was gone, maybe just knocked out. I tried to check her pulse, but there was nothing there."

It all made sense. The footsteps I'd seen weren't two people physically fighting, it was one person trying to save another one, but it went terribly wrong. It was possible that fall immediately damaged Elise's brain and she died nearly instantly.

"I had to think fast, so I ran to the pool house, grabbed some chlorine tablets and put them in her mouth, holding it closed so maybe it would trickle down to her stomach and *this asshole*," Peter pointed to Scott, "would go to prison."

"*I'm* the asshole?" Scott blurted out. His face was turning red, enraged at what he'd just heard. "You killed Elise and tried to frame me but *I'm* the asshole here. Why you son of a—" before Sheriff Jackson had a chance to grab him this time, Scott ran at Peter who was still sitting on the ground. I got out of my squatting stance just in time before Scott tackled Peter back down to the ground, once again nearly crushing Jessica.

"Hey!" Jessica shouted in as much surprise as pain. "That's enough!"

Scott had Peter by the collar and was slamming him against the ground and Jessica's trapped leg. The whole scene seemed ridiculous considering that Peter had just told us that head trauma had killed Mrs. Huntington-Wilbury.

Sheriff Jackson ran behind Scott and was easily able to lift him off of Peter, who sat up and shook his head, trying to get his bearings again. Jessica escaped and moved to the side, out of harm's way once and for all. I went over to make sure she was okay, but while my back was turned, this time Peter got a second wind and stood up, charging at both Scott and Sheriff Jackson.

Despite seeming a little frail, Peter hit them like a wrecking ball and they went tumbling to the ground. Peter landed on Scott, his main target, and began punching him, though it didn't look like there was much power behind the punches. In fact, he seemed to be getting weaker by the second. From behind the melee, I could see Peter's body convulsing and I ran over to see why. The gardener was sitting on top of Scott, sobbing yet again.

Then suddenly there was a loud sound from the hedges behind them, and something burst through. It was Muffy! She was barking and jumped on top of Peter, biting him until he got off Scott. It wasn't play biting, but it wasn't biting to kill either.

Peter rolled off and laid flat on his back. Muffy moved to my side and then pointed her nose and front foot at Peter. "Good girl," I patted her head and she released her rigid stance.

The gardener sat up, extended his hands in front of him and blurted, "Take me in, Sheriff! I can't handle this anymore." Then he kept loudly wailing and all of us rolled our eyes.

Scott pushed himself up to standing with a grunt. There were grass stains on his boardshorts.

Sheriff Jackson had finally pushed himself up to sitting on his butt, resting back on his hands, watching this bizarre scene unfold.

Peter flopped onto his back, hands still outstretched in front of him, pointing straight into the air now. "What are you waiting for?" he cried.

I nodded to Sheriff Jackson, wordlessly telling him to get over there. Sheriff Jackson came to his senses and leaned forward, grabbing the cuffs from his belt and putting them on Peter's wrists. But Peter didn't move, he just layed there, hands outstretched.

"This guy sucks," Scott said, looking down at Peter, then began to walk away.

"Not so fast," Sheriff Jackson said, hopping up and grabbing Scott by the shoulder. "You still have some questions to answer."

Chapter 42

"You've got to be kidding me," Scott moaned. "Like what? You already know who did it. He just admitted to everything. I'm free to go."

"I need to know why you didn't tell us about your tell-all book deal. It could have helped us piece things together faster if you had. That *could* be seen as obstruction of justice," Sheriff Jackson explained. I knew the evidence they had against Scott would never hold water in a court, but I also suspected that Scott *didn't* know that.

"Isn't it obvious?" Scott sighed, clearly exhausted from everything surrounding this murder. "If I told you, I would have looked even more guilty. That public defender you got me told me I should have told you, but what does he know? And besides, wouldn't that have made you look harder at me and not at anyone else?"

It was a logical argument. I'd certainly thought he was more guilty once I'd learned the information.

"I suppose that's a possibility," Sheriff Jackson agreed. "But the next time you have a lawyer, you should listen to what they say, for the sake of everyone involved."

"Hopefully there isn't a next time," Scott added. "So can I go or what?"

Sheriff Jackson looked at me and I gave a slight shrug, indicating I had nothing else to ask. "Yup, that'll do it," he said.

Scott gave us all a salute and walked away, out of the maze. "See ya later, idiots."

Muffy growled at Scott as he passed. I patted her on the head.

"Now what do we do with this guy?" Jessica asked, pointing down at Peter who was still crying in the same prone position.

Sheriff Jackson thought for a minute, then said, "I don't see there's much that we can do."

That quieted Peter who had somehow been able to hear through his loud sobs. He didn't move but sniffled and asked, "What do you mean? I admitted I did it."

"Yeah, how can you just ignore that?" Jessica asked.

I explained, "A confession alone isn't always enough to convict someone."

"A confession is important, but there needs to be some kind of evidence," Sheriff Jackson continued. "All that we have is the tablet wrapper, a dead body, and a story that explains those. But it very well could still have been Scott. There's nothing concrete to specifically tie Peter to the murder."

"Me!" Peter exclaimed. "I'm tying myself to the murder!" He got up with some difficulty thanks to the cuffs that were on his wrists.

"Even with your confession, it's unlikely they have enough to charge you with third degree manslaughter," Sheriff Jackson explained. "That charge means it was an accident. You could get up to 20 years in prison and maybe a fine. Or maybe nothing. It all depends on what they want to charge you with. We have means and opportunity, but motive is a little weak. And none of that really matters because it's all circumstantial."

Peter was confused. "Who is 'they'?"

"Oh, this case is out of my hands now. Since Ms. Huntington-Wilbury was such a, uh, *prominent* member of the community, the county has taken the case. But with the lack of evidence, the high number of backlogged cases they already have, and the surprising lack of press this has gotten, I'd be surprised if they pursue it."

Peter looked like he was about to break out into sobs again, so I hurriedly added, "But I'm sure the sheriff will take you down to the station and hold you there until they decide what the best way forward is." I tried to urge Sheriff Jackson with my eyes, hoping he'd pick up on the hint. Sometimes when people felt guilty enough, they wanted to atone for what they'd done.

He did, and said, "Oh, um, yeah. Get up, Mr. Flowers. I'm taking you down to the station to make a statement." Unfortunately this had the opposite effect that I thought it would and Peter started crying again. I figured if he got what he wanted — to be arrested — he'd stop his blubbering. But through his gasps, we could hear him saying, "Okay, Sheriff Jackson! I don't want to get locked up but I will cooperate! I'm coming with you willingly!"

Jessica muttered, "Oh, brother," under her breath. I had to stifle a laugh. Sheriff Jackson led Peter out of the hedged-in area of the maze and turned a corner disappearing from sight. "Could he have been any more dramatic?"

Both of us finally let out the laughs we'd been holding in. Then a jolt of panic hit me and I jumped to my feet. "Jess, do you remember how to get out of here?"

A look of panic crossed over Jessica's face as she hopped up shouting, "NO!"

Chapter 43

We both ran out into the maze with Muffy at our heels, turning the way that Sheriff Jackson had turned earlier. The fog had grown thicker, making it much darker outside than it should have been at this time of the day. We stopped at the next turn in the maze and were quiet. We could just hear Peter's wailing loud enough to follow his voice and laughed to ourselves again. To my relief, we finally tumbled out of the maze just as we saw Sheriff Jackson and Peter disappear in the fog, walking towards Sheriff Jackson's car.

Out in the field, for some reason the fog was clearing and we looked around the yard. Muffy ran circles in the grass, getting out some of her never-ending energy. "Is it messed up of us to laugh at Peter?" I asked Jessica as she sat down on the grass. I followed her lead, plopping down and letting the adrenaline in my system settle. I felt bad for the gardener, but there was something amusing about how over-the-top his reaction was.

"Let's just say if he were on an acting audition, he wouldn't get the part," Jessica answered and both started laughing again.

Then out of the corner of my eye, I saw Melinda walking towards us. She was carrying a bag of takeout food and a bouquet of store-bought tulips in their plastic wrapping. I nudged Jessica and we both stopped laughing and waved at her. With no free hands, she waved using the bouquet.

Once Melinda walked across enough of the grass lawn for us to hear her, she said, "What the heck just happened? I saw the Sheriff driving off with someone in the backseat, but the person's head was down. Who was it!? Is that who killed my aunt?"

She arrived at the spot where we were sitting just as she finished asking her questions. "Come join us," Jessica patted the grass next to her indicating where Melinda should sit, and she followed directions, setting her bag and flowers down, and putting her legs to the side in a refined seated stance instead of the more casual criss-crossed legs.

"That was Peter," I let out the breath I didn't realize I'd been holding in and answered her questions. "And yes, he's the one who killed your aunt. I'm so sorry to have to tell you that."

"Peter?!" Melinda exclaimed. "Gentle, old Peter? No..." She put her hand to her chest indicating that she was genuinely surprised by this news. "That can't be true. He was always my favorite member of the staff. Ever since I was a girl he'd clip a little rose for me whenever I came to visit Auntie Elise."

I was studying Melinda's reaction to see if there was any hint of falseness in it, but there wasn't. She seemed genuinely surprised, though not that broken up. "Yeah, he admitted to the whole thing. But it was an accident."

Melinda quietly nodded her head. I wondered how much disappointment one person could take before they broke. Melinda seemed to be able to shoulder more than most. Seizing the opportunity, Jessica jumped in, "Do you want to know everything or just the basics?"

"Well, I suppose I should know everything. Hold on, let me get this out," Melinda pulled a bottle of red wine out of the bag she'd been carrying and a wine key to open it out of her purse. I didn't know the difference between wines aside from their color, but I assumed it was a good one if Melinda chose it. "Auntie Elise didn't have anything to uncork a bottle of wine. At least not one that I could find. There's just so much *stuff* in there," she said, successfully uncorking the bottle with a squeaky POP! as she said "stuff." She took a swig, then took one more. "Ahh, that's better. You want some?" She offered the bottle to both me and Jessica.

Jessica gently took the bottle from Melinda. "Considering this is my favorite wine, *yes*! Thanks," and took a swig then handed it back.

"Okay, I'm ready," Melinda said, knocking back one more large drink.

I started explaining, "There's no delicate way to put this but you should probably know, your aunt was sleeping with almost all of the male staff members here."

"WHAT?!" Melinda exclaimed, nearly knocking over the bottle of wine. "That can't be true."

"Trust us, it is," Jessica said, then waved her hand urging me to go on. "It got complicated."

"Scott was one of them—" I went on but Melinda interrupted me.

"Eww, Auntie, no! Not Scott. Gross. Sorry Tawny, keep going," Melinda grimaced and apologized for the outburst.

Unfazed, I continued. "Well, he got offered a deal from a publisher to write a tell-all about your aunt. They were interested in her rich, reclusive lifestyle. He was telling Lady Sinclair about it—"

"— who was also sleeping with Scott —" Jessica interjected and Melinda made a gagging sound.

I continued. "— and Peter overheard," I paused to give Melinda a chance to ask questions, but she just looked straight ahead, her eyes already starting to glaze over thanks to the wine. "Peter was in a *very* long-term relationship with your aunt. Probably before you were born."

"That must have been why he was always so thoughtful when you were a kid," Jessica added as she reached for the bottle to take another drink.

"Mmmhmm," Melinda nodded in agreement. "This is already a lot to process but keep going. I'm going to shut up so you can tell me everything at once and I'll know how much I have to react to."

"Okay, but only if you're sure you're fine?" I asked and Melinda nodded. "Anyways, Peter found your aunt in the maze the day of the party. He tried to tell her that he knew about her relationship with Scott and to warn her that Scott was abusing it to make money off of her. They fought, Peter fell, your aunt tried to catch him, but she fell too and hit her head. She wasn't responsive. So Peter saw it as a chance to frame Scott by using the chlorine tablets, since as he sees it, Scott ruined both his life *and* his romance with your aunt."

"And that's it?" Melinda asked after I paused.

"Yup, a pretty simple case once it broke down," I responded.

Melinda was quiet for a minute. Then Jessica broke the silence asking, "Guess that means you and Dario are free to live happily ever after now, right?" I suspected she'd been mulling over this question for awhile but the liquid courage finally gave her the push she needed to ask it.

"No way," Melinda rolled her eyes. "I don't think I'll ever talk to him again. At least not without a lawyer present."

I was surprised by this strong move. I'd assumed lovelorn Melinda would stick it out and try to make it work with Dario, and I started to think I'd underestimated her.

"I told him to get out as soon as we got home from the Sheriff's Station. Who knows where he is now. Probably dreaming up another scam," she waved her hand in the air.

"Are you going to sue him?" Jessica asked, maybe a bit too eagerly.

"Honestly, I haven't mentally gotten that far yet. I'm just proud of myself for little things, like going out to get dinner while all of this is going on, you know? Instead of wallowing at home." As she said this, Melinda seemed more self-assured than I'd ever seen her over the last few days. "Frankly though, I'd be fine if I never saw or heard from him again."

"That's the spirit!" Jessica added. "So what are you doing with all of this?" Jessica gestured to the house and the grass they were sitting on. Muffy was laying in the middle of the yard having worn herself out for the moment.

Melinda thought before answering. "I'm going to keep it. I've been wandering around for a long time, and I think that I want to stick around here for a while. It might be nice to put down some roots. To have something to call my own."

The answer surprised me, and I hadn't realized until that moment that I was a little sad at the potential of Melinda moving. We had struck up a kind of friendship over the last few days, and I didn't want to see her go back to the lonely life of travel she was on before. There were more than enough places to take influencer pictures here at the estate and in Shantytown. "That's great news!" I said.

"Actually, Tawny," Melinda turned towards me. "I was wondering if you can handle taking on another client? I need a more active routine and I'd love to train with you."

"Tawny is the *best*," Jessica gushed, making me blush.

"I'd love to train you!" I said. "Let me know when you're free and I'll make a personalized plan."

We all fell into silence for a moment, taking in the beauty of the place where we were sitting, watching the fog slowly shift around and start to dissipate. I realized I'd never been here before when it was this quiet.

There were birds chirping even though I couldn't see them, a cool breeze blowing, and somewhere in the distance there was a fountain gently running. It was the most peaceful I'd felt in a long time.

Then like a bat out of hell, Muffy came barreling right into me. I hadn't even heard her sneak up on me. I laughed and petted her as she licked me.

"Muffy! Get off her!" Melinda shouted, shooing the dog away from me. But I kept petting her.

"I've got to admit, I'm going to miss my run-ins with Muffy," I said.

"Well, to be honest with you, I don't know what to do with her. She has a mind of her own and way too much energy for me. I don't want to send her to a shelter, but she'll just become feral out here," Melinda sighed, knocking back another swig of wine.

An idea popped in my head and before I had a chance to talk myself out of it I said, "What if I take her?"

"You?!" Melinda and Jessica asked in unison.

"Yeah! It's not that crazy," I defended myself. "I've been thinking about getting a dog to go running with, for protection, and companionship in general." As I said this, Muffy settled down next to me and put her head in my lap.

"I mean, yeah, that would be best for *me*," Melinda said. "But you're *positive* you want her? She's kind of a handful."

I thought about it for a second. "I'm positive."

With that settled, Jessica blurted, "Well, I have to get home. I was supposed to be back in L.A. tonight, but how could I pass up the opportunity to catch a killer," she asked in a way that made it clear it was a hypothetical question.

"I guess that means I'm leaving too because I'm your ride. Oops, I mean, *we're* your ride," I said as I nodded to Muffy, getting up and brushing myself off, then reaching my hand out to Melinda to help her up to her feet too.

Melinda looked a little surprised. "I know how silly this is going to sound, but I think you two are the best friends I've ever had in my adult life."

That did surprise me, in a way that made me feel very sad for Melinda, but was also endearing. "I'm glad we're friends, too," I hugged her.

Jessica, Muffy, and I walked with Melinda to the back door of the house. "You sure you're going to be okay here by yourself?" Jessica asked as Melinda walked inside through the French doors in the backyard.

Melinda looked around inside, then smiled. "Yeah. I think I'm going to be better than okay."

"Hey, one more thing," Jessica said, halting Melinda from closing the door. "I'm just curious, what are you going to do about Peter?"

I poked Jessica in the rib for asking a question like that right after finding out he killed Melinda's aunt.

"You know, I think I'll keep him on if they don't lock him up. I think I'll probably keep everyone on; they're kind of like family. Except for Scott of course. He's the worst," Melinda said.

"The absolute worst, right?" Jessica asked.

"Drive safe, ladies. Hopefully the next time we hang out, it's for fun," Melinda laughed then closed the back door.

We started walking back to my car, which looked out of place at such a grand home. "I really like Melinda," Jessica said. "We're going to hang out with her more, right?"

"As much as I hate the drive up here, yeah, I think we're all genuine friends now," I smiled.

"Do you think you'll ever tell her about secretly recording her?" Jessica asked.

That fact had been nagging at me ever since I realized I actually liked Melinda as a person. "I'm sure I will when there's a good time. Though I have a feeling she won't really care that much. She might be the most forgiving, understanding person I've ever met."

"Yeah, I bet that's true," Jessica said, and stumbled while getting into the car, the wine buzz fully hitting her now. "Whoa! I need water, ASAP. Just take me home. I'll have

Lloyd drive me down to get my car tomorrow morning and I'll leave super early for the city."

"Not a problem, but you'll have to give me directions," I opened up the back door for Muffy and she hopped right in and sat down, like she'd been riding back there for years. Then I started up my car and started rolling down the driveway. It only took a couple of minutes before Jessica had fallen asleep in the passenger seat. But she was awakened by my phone ringing.

"Huh, that's weird," I commented.

"Who is it?" Jessica groggily asked.

"It's Lady Sinclair. She normally doesn't call unless she's canceling an appointment last minute, but we don't have one until next week."

"Well, answer it!" Jessica urged, the crime-solving bug clearly not quite out of her system yet.

"Hello?" I answered, then put it on speakerphone, but raised my finger to my lips, indicating to Jessica to be quiet.

"Tawny, it's Lady Sinclair. I have some news for you," she said, and didn't even wait for me to respond before continuing on. "Scott has left Shantytown. Permanently."

Jessica I exchanged curious looks. "Oh? Did he tell you that or did you see him packing up or something?" I asked.

"He called to tell me he was taking the tell-all book deal. Apparently the price went up since poor Elise died in such a *scandalous* manner," Lady Sinclar explained.

"I'm sure Melinda's lawyers will have something to say about it," I said. "She likely owns Elise's life rights."

"Yes, of course," Lady Sinclair said and I noticed she sounded a little melancholy. Could it be possible that she missed Scott?

"Are you okay, Lady Sinclair?" I asked after there were a few moments of silence.

Lady Sinclair sighed on the other end. "Tawny, my dear, I am *always* okay. I just thought you'd want to know."

"Well thank you for telling me. I was definitely interested in what his next move would be," I affirmed. When Lady Sinclair didn't say anything but didn't hang up either, I asked, "Is there anything else?"

"Actually, I was wondering if you had time for a session tomorrow. Maybe something around 11 a.m.?" Lady Sinclair asked.

I smiled, realizing this was her way of reaching out for companionship now that her former lover was out of the picture. I didn't need to check my schedule. I'd find a way to make sure she wasn't alone longer than she wanted to be. "That works! And in case you want something sooner, I can squeeze you in this evening," I offered.

Lady Sinclair jumped at the opportunity. "I'd love that! I'll see you at 7 p.m." she said then hung up.

"Tawny, why are you so nice to that woman? She's miserable and she's mean to everyone," Jessica dragged out the last word to get her point across.

Thank you!

Thank you for reading this Tawny Monroe Mystery! I hope you enjoyed it! If you could take a couple of seconds and rate this book, I'd be so grateful!

As an independent author, your reviews and ratings make all of the difference!

I appreciate you!

Natalie

About the author

Natalie Saar is a journalist and author who is passionate about creating stories that inspire and entertain. She's the author of *Becoming 1% Better*, a nonfiction guide to personal growth, and psychological thrillers like *Do What I Say*, *Attack*, and *Stalker*.

After three years of planning, writing, and rewriting, in September 2025, Natalie launched the Tawny Monroe Mystery series, a cozy, twist-filled journey through small-town secrets and clever puzzles.

As the founder of The Indie Authors, she also helps writers publish and thrive. Guided by her mantra —"Make someone feel special today"—Natalie continues to empower readers and writers alike, one story at a time.

Other works

You can find other works by Natalie at all major etailers. If you want to connect, she can be reached at nataliesaar.com.

Series

Tawny Monroe Mystery

Steeped in Murder (A Tawny Monroe Mystery)
Cooking up Murder (A Tawny Monroe Mystery)

Paranomaly Podcast Mystery

Finding Frogman

Standalone stories

Becoming 1% Better

Do What I Say

Attack

Stalker